BLACK

RIVER

RUN

BLACK RIVER RUN

A Novel

Kiran Khalap

AMARYLLIS

AMARYLLIS

An imprint of Manjul Publishing House Pvt. Ltd.
•7/32, Ansari Road, Daryaganj, New Delhi 110 002
Website: www.manjulindia.com

Registered Office:
•10, Nishat Colony, Bhopal 462 003 – India

Copyright © Kiran Khalap, 2019

This edition first published in 2019

ISBN 978-93-88241-93-9

Cover design by Supriya Saran

Printed and bound in India by Thomson Press (India) Ltd.

For
Rajashree Khalap, my life partner since 1987, who
reintroduced me to universes I had lost touch with since
childhood

Thanks to friend Sekhar Chandrasekhar who introduced me to Worli BDD chawls and to his friend, Inspector Yeshwant Phatak, who explained the riots there

Contents

Author's Note

The theatre of action in the novel *Black River Run* is the iconic Worli BDD Chawls.

The protagonist, affectionately known as Buva, is a member of the lowest or untouchable caste in the caste system of India. He has been orphaned by members of the upper caste in a tiny village and has been brought to the BDD Chawls in Mumbai. Even here, he experiences the violent friction between the two factions.

Here is a short note to explain the significance of the BDD Chawls as well as the riots that have regularly affected the social fabric of India's most cosmopolitan city.

The iconic BDD Chawls

The acronym BDD refers to British Development Directorate (or Department), who built these buildings in the 1920s. They were originally meant to be prisons for the rising number of Indian freedom fighters, but over time got converted into residential tenements. The 195 buildings could house over 50,000 Mumbaikars.

Rumour has it that in a city that gets over 240 cm of rainfall during its famed monsoons, the only buildings that do not experience water seepage are the BDD chawls, since their walls are prison-thick!

They were built at four locations in Mumbai: Parel, Worli, Sewri and Naigaon, of which Worli has the largest cluster of 121 buildings.

'Chawl' is a word from Marathi, the language of the inhabitants of Mumbai.

One learned Marathi poet hypothesised that 'chawl' itself could have emerged from the Marathi word 'saal' meaning verandah or from 'chaal' meaning walk, since a chawl is characterised by the wide central corridor with rooms on either side.

Chawls, unlike the modern skyscrapers mushrooming in Mumbai, represented communities, since most homes never closed their front doors and the inhabitants moved freely between families. The community provided a sense of shared ownership of children, who found warmth and succour in an adopted 'aunt' or 'uncle' when their own parents grew testy. In moments of crises, the community extended help and hope both.

Multiple governments have attempted to redevelop the chawls since 2004. After several bureaucratic hiccups, Lower Parel and Naigaon were handed over to private developers for redevelopment in 2017. Worli's fate has not been decided.

Next to Worli BDD Chawls is the famed Jamboree Maidan, where Mumbaikars congregated during the freedom movement (started in 1885) to listen to national leaders, and during the mill-strikes created by the labour movement between 1960 and 1980 to listen to predominantly leftist leaders.

Today, the Jamboree Maidan is famous for, arguably, the tallest 'dahi handi' in South Mumbai. The festival of the birth of Lord Krishna, who would steal dahi (yogurt) from a handi (mud-pot) hanging from the ceiling, recreates this scenario: the handi is hung fairly high above an open space and teams of youngsters attempt to reach it by creating human pyramids.

The Guinness Book of World Records acknowledged the record of a pyramid as high as 43.79 feet, created by a group named Govinda in 2012, breaking a Spanish group's record of 39.27 feet!

The riots of Mumbai

Like all great port cities of the world, Mumbai (called Bombay till 1995) is a melting pot of cultures, communities, religions, languages, lifestyles.

The differences have more often than not co-existed peacefully.

And yet, it is idealistic to hope that there would never be friction. Mumbai has witnessed riots between Parsis and Muslims, Hindus and Muslims, upper-caste Hindus and Dalits (or the lowest caste of Hindus) and between gangs owned by drug lords and smugglers.

While the 1992-93 riots between Hindus and Muslims after the demolition of the Babri Masjid, with over 700 deaths, are often referred to as 'The Bombay Riots', the 1972 riots marked a seismic shift in the relationship between the 'untouchable' Dalits and the rest of the Hindus.

The riots confirmed the rise of the Dalit Panther movement, on the lines of the Black Panther movement in the US, that challenged the supremacy of the whites.

Ironically, 1972 also marked the twenty-fifth year of Indian independence from the British, thus confirming that very little had changed in the caste system in over two decades. Atrocities continued to be perpetrated especially against Dalit women not just in Maharashtra, but in other states of India.

The Worli BDD Chawls were the epicentre of these riots.

Close to 20,000 Dalits emerged from the shadows, against police orders, who, once the situation got beyond control, fired bullets that ended up killing eleven Dalits.

The Black Panther movement gathered steam in Mumbai as well as other regions, but the Emergency declared in 1977 probably nipped it in the bud.

Today, the Dalit movement is represented more by the socio-political movement of Neo-Buddhism, named after the renowned Dalit Babasaheb Ambedkar, known as the Father of the Indian Constitution, who converted to Buddhism in 1956.

One

Buva and a Broken Door

His deltoid bulged shamelessly and popped out of the half-sleeve of his white terry-cotton safari-suit top. At the sound of the rip, his body froze in a half-curve as he swung on the pockmarked iron of the parallel bar, also known as 'double bar' among the local gang of exercisers at Shri Bhogadevi Sports Club, while another half-curve broke across his face.

It was 6 a.m.

Buva has finished his twenty-four surya namaskars, the yoga routine that characterised his hero Swami Samarth

Ramdas, and is applying the finishing touches to his physical regimen.

He has chanted the twelve names of the Sun God in his mind as he held each of the twelve poses of a surya namaskar, and he has begun the entire exercise with the famous Gayatri mantra.

That his deltoids have progressed well in mimicking Swami Samarth Ramdas's brought a rare grin to Buva's face, but it also delayed him for work, since he had to sew up the sleeve himself as a proud, independent bachelor.

He is late to start 'Kamandalu', his Premier Padmini cab, which reduces his record of timeliness from 300 to 299 days out of the 365 days. Kamandalu, meaning 'begging bowl' in common parlance, is written in the seven colours of the rainbow on the rear windshield of his cab (Chassis number XM824764XOX).

He is not very sure if he is pleased or angry with himself. He strokes his rich black beard in indecision. No strands come off; his white safari-suit top remains untroubled by black question marks.

I am a knife. I am a knife that cuts through the illusions of life.

Buva soaks up the world through his senses.

Just as his mind needs the *Dasbodh*, the masterly treatise on how to balance the life of action and contemplation by

Swami Samarth Ramdas, the skin needs food, as do the eyes and the ears and the tongue.

He smiles to himself when he thinks of Reshma's soft, tickly, black waterfall of hair on his stomach and her tongue on… hmmm… haven't sat with her for many months, or is it years, now?

'Sitting' is a euphemism in the Worli BDD chawls, in Congress House, in Kamathipura, areas that feed female flesh to male, islands in the nation that are unconnected to the English nation called India.

The English speakers are just about 120 million strong in a swarming sea of 1.2 billion Indians.

The English nation is defined by the Eye.

Eyes have eyelids. So Eyes can choose not to see.

The Eye reads, watches, absorbs, and writes proposals, agreements and PowerPoint presentations in great detail and sometimes idiomatic English, and replies via email.

It has soaked up a spectrum of ideas from Adam Smith to Thorstein Veblen, been seduced both by the Beatles and Beethoven, Botticelli and M.F. Husain, hummus and wasabi, and single malt whisky and Oxford Street fashion.

It has cut off the umbilical cord to its mother tongue, and along with it, to one of the most advanced civilisations in the history of humankind.

It has no clue about the Indian calendar, as opposed

to the Gregorian calendar of Sunday, and January, and it is probably unaware that there are over six different such calendars in the country, and therefore, its synapses with the movement of the sun and the moon, because it's a lunisolar calendar, with the changing seasons, with the changing festivals every week and month, have been singed and destroyed.

The inhabitants have vague notions about the Other Nation, which in turn has no clue about the Eye nation.

The Other Nation is broken up by many languages, each with a separate tit to suckle, each with its own supply of milk sinuses flowing out of aureoles of bhajans and kirtans and shlokas and holy men dispensing advice.

The Other Nation is driven by the Ear.

Ears have no lids, so Ears cannot choose to not hear.

Listen to others, discuss, argue, shout, make the music louder, speak on the mobile phone for so long the nation becomes a world leader in 'number of talk minutes per person'.

All communication in this Ear Nation is in rhymes, be it reminders for polio vaccine or tax payments by the government or condoms by private enterprises.

They have no patience with instruction manuals, business agreements or minutes of the meeting.

The Ear Nation is a slave to the Indian calendar.

You can eat only vegetarian food on Monday, Wednesday and Friday, and you can eat non-vegetarian food, that is, eggs and fish and meat, only on Tuesdays, Thursdays and Saturdays, or vice versa, depending on which calendar you follow and which part of India you are from, because this day is for this goddess, who bestows long life, and that day is for that god, who keeps your children out of harm's way, and Saturday is for Lord Shani, who prevents bones from being broken.

Both Indias coexist in a Mumbai carved out by twenty million human beings who pursue a whore called fame and a popsicle called money under a sky that is a muggy bell jar.

The two Indias intersect twice a day, without shaking hands, and their eyes rarely meet.

One hides guilt; the other, anger.

They even travel up to their vertical theatres of work by separate lifts, in order to avoid a contamination of body odours and ideas. In some cruel arenas, the women and men have to climb up the stairs even to the tenth floor.

The Eye nation tries every trick to build moats between itself and the Ear nation.

Their tides are governed by the sun, not the moon.

First, at daybreak, when the women from the slums migrate to the houses of the rich as housemaids, dog-walkers, last-night's-binge-drinking-puke cleaners, cooks, garbage-throwers, nurses of sick fathers and mothers unwanted in their childlike state of incontinence and glazed stares, buyers of fruit and vegetables and kolam rice, feeders of children as young as five months since the mother is chasing her vice-presidentship in a bank, and in some cases, upholders of the libidos of ageing Lotharios.

The male tide drifts in as drivers of cars: they drive postage-stamp-sized Maruti 800s and the growling new Audis and muscular new SUVs for their employers, ferry the housemaids with their belongings including employer's kids to the schools or cabbages back from the bazaars, but always, their lives, like Buva's, are governed by the tar rivers of Mumbai.

Then, as the sun lowers itself in the brown Arabian Sea, just for a few moments creating an impossibly golden sherbet spilt on the horizon, the slum dwellers switch on their TVs, and through the luminescence braided out of red-blue-green pixels, they download the dreams of the other India.

They goggle at nymphets stilettoing through corridors or youth with six-pack abs riding motorbikes of thigh-numbing power.

On this screen, nobody sleeps in crumpled clothes; they lay down their heads unencumbered by solid gold tiaras and bodies mummified in expensive silk.

The biggest divide between the two Indias, though, is not visible to the eye.

It runs along the thousands of receptors in the nose.

The Eye Nation floats in crisp, fresh, spring-flower smells let loose by minimally packaged perfumes and deodorants sold by petulant, anorexic women staring out of billboards next to glass-covered box buildings; the Ear Nation loves heavy, heady smells swirling out of glass bottles of oils and lotions.

Buva ferries human beings from one India to the other.

'Chanel Number Five?' His eyes meet the young woman's in the rear-view mirror as she slides into the back seat of his cab at Worli Naka without bothering to ask him.

My nose is a ruthless hunter.

'No… Colaba.' She is too distracted; the question is out of context.

'Scent, scent… Chanel Number Five?' he asks, his left deltoid once again stretching his wounded white tericot sleeve as he reaches out of the front window and twists the Argo taximeter's neck upside down, while his right hand taps his nostril, unable as he is to express himself with clarity in the language of the Eye Nation.

The woman's eyes widen in surprise when she understands his question, realising he has substituted 'sh' with 'ch' in the pronunciation of the perfume brand.

She smiles in reply. Her eyebrows are arched like a bow above kohl-lined eyes. Long eyelashes—nowadays they use fake ones, Reshma had told him.

Tight smile. Why?

Crisp white linen shirt and a short denim skirt. Her fingers tap a soundless rhythm on her brown leather purse placed in her lap.

She is going to meet someone and is undecided about her plan of action.

'What time do you want to reach?' Buva always asks his passengers this question.

That information allows him to choose the road most suitable to travel along the six vital meridians of Mumbai.

'Fast.'

The time taken is not for travel; it's for the traffic signals. The actual distances within Mumbai are small.

It's 10.30 a.m.

The woman winds up the windscreen on her side. Doesn't want her hair to look awry—she must be going to meet someone important.

They finally reach Colaba. 'I'll go and get the money... don't have change... from my friend...' the young lady informs him.

Voice still strangled. Poor thing must be carrying a thorny battle inside her heart.

8

He pulls out the pocket edition of the *Dasbodh* as he waits for her in the dappled lane—3rd Pasta Lane in Colaba.

Colaba was one of the last of the seven islands of Mumbai to be connected to the others, granted in dowry to the English by the Portuguese.

Colaba has the highest number of representatives of both Eye and Ear nation. The Bakhtavar Building at Colaba Post Office, also referred to as the Chairmen's Building, and opposite it the Sea Wind of the Ambanis house heads of organisations whose net worth exceeds that of the rest of Mumbai.

A stone's throw away are the sprawling slums of Ganesh Murti Nagar.

Buva often wonders about how places in Mumbai got their names. He can understand Walkeshwar because Lord Ram's idol was made of sand, and thus a compound word for Sand and Lord, and Chunabhatti, because they manufactured chuna or lime there in bhattis or kilns, but why Pasta?

Buva has no clue that it was a title granted to a family by the British, and what would he do with such information?

Whatever its name means, the lane is a calmative drug.

Smells of succulent Sindhi food drift out, fragrant flags of the most fundamental human need. A geriatric motor in the lubricant-slithery garage coughs rhythmically. A warm sun bounces off the black skin of the cab, the shadows shaking along with the restless ficus leaves that filter it.

The Argo taximeter ticks away, counting money in its own currency of gears revolving so many times a minute. Nothing less than the best for Buva. New meter brands like Super and Diamond were cheaper by fifty percent, but he refused to switch from Argo. It was always less expensive in the long run.

'*Jyacha jyacha jo vyaapaar, thethe asaave khabardaar, duschitpane tari por, vedha laavi,*' the *Dasbodh* had said this morning.

'In your own job be alert, or even a child can deceive you.'

He snaps out of his reverie.

Where is my money?

Where is she?

She said she was getting it from her friend.

Buva gets out of the Premier Padmini, pulls the keys out and walks over to the security guard, who is getting his ear cleaned by a leather-bag-carrying ear specialist.

'Did you see that woman... white shirt... she owes me money!'

The security guard, unlike most caricatures employed in these posh areas, is brawny and moustachioed. Shiny black shoes, neatly parted hair. His otherwise impressive personality is currently compromised by the look on his face:

he has an orgasmic lopsided grin twisted in the direction of the particular ear being dredged for its sewage. He points to the B entrance and holds out three limp fingers, as the ear-cleaning expert digs deeper with singular purpose.

Old building, wooden handrail, polished mosaic steps, neatly finished with three decorative lines indicating the end of each step. Plastic mango leaf toran on flat 3, floor 1; rangoli patterns outside flat 4, floor 2.

You could have been a detective, you old goon.

All the four flats on the 3rd floor are locked. There are padlocks of varying weight on their latches. Did the security guard not say 3rd floor?

The light is subaqueous despite the brightness of the sun outside. Someone had the bright idea of painting the window panes in the corridor dark.

Buva hears a short strangled cry.

He straightens up. Honed over the multiple gang wars in BDD chawls, his senses reach a funambulist's tautness; he is walking a high-wire between two peaks of a tension. He tiptoes to each door. With a shock, he realises that one of the padlocks is a dummy: the lock is on the stem of a latch that has been sawed off so that a casual glance cannot reveal the subterfuge.

Buva rings the bell.

There is a sound of feet shuffling.

11

The opening strains of the title music for *Kaamgaar Sabha*, the Marathi music radio programme for mill workers, escapes from the floor above.

Must be 11 a.m.

A sheet of cold air leaks out of the door.

The air conditioner was on.

Rich owner obviously.

Outside the building, a loudspeaker starts blaring a bhajan.

The door opens a fraction. A curly-haired man with bloodshot eyes peers over the door's security chain. He was barrel-chested and muscular, with a red-and-white striped towel around a hard, bulging midriff.

'What do you want?' he asks with aggression that gets tempered into irritation by the sight of someone bigger than him.

'My money, 105 rupees... taxi (Buva reverentially touches his triangular brass badge)... woman came here?'

'No. Go away.'

Unfortunately for Curly Head, Buva is almost a foot taller than him. Over his head, he sees, just before the door is slammed shut, a sliver of a sight that freezes his blood.

The woman from the cab has dragged out the chair she is tied to, hands behind her back, one leg to the leg of the chair. The kohl around the eyes has run down her cheeks, the twin streams of black bracketing the bank notes stuffed in her mouth. Her white shirt is unbuttoned, and her fleshy breasts have popped out of a dehiscent bra.

For a fraction of a second, her eyes widen in recognition.

Buva clenches his fists. This is none of your business. This is between girl and boy, husband and wife, man and woman—you hear its pitiful echoes every night in the feculent holes-in-the-wall called BDD chawls.

Some men drag their women by their hair, some brand them with cigarette butts; this one has tied her up to a chair and gagged her.

Walk away; this is none of your business.'

This is my business. I need my money. 105 bucks is not a joke. It is half the cost of a full tank of CNG.

Buva rings the bell again.

No response.

He rings it once more.

I miss my iron bar. I should have carried my iron bar. What if there is a need to fight?

He remembers the flesh he lost in that fight in Antop Hill.

Maybe Curly Head has realised the truth of Buva's claim.

Maybe he will give me 105 rupees and end the misery of my indecision.

The door opens this time, but what is visible is the

barrel of a pistol, its steel mouth as if open to whistle, in line with Buva's solar plexus.

Wish I had my iron bar.

Buva strokes his beard as he walks the serrated edge of indecision.

Curly Head smirks.

'Fuck off. Nikal jao.'

Curly Head has misunderstood, misread, misinterpreted.

A metallic ting is triggered in Buva's temple.

Buva steps back twice, out of the line of fire, and before Curly Head can latch the door, hurls himself at it.

When a one hundred and seventy-five centimetre tall man weighing seventy-five kilograms with well-developed musculature hits a door at an angry speed, a loosely attached chain is unlikely to hold.

Buva is surprised by the impact of his dash, but he is the first to get upright. His urgency is unnecessary.

Curly Head has probably banged the back of his head as the door slammed him to the floor. He appears unconscious, lying on his back, the towel askew, exposing a glistening, turgid penis. He is breathing heavily.

The pistol is lying near the woman's feet, and the door is still open.

Buva slams the door shut.

He picks up the pistol.

Bloody hell, nobody in BDD chawls has seen such a sophisticated weapon, only the police have.

Maybe Prakash knows—Prakash who rose from the muck of the chawls to become a police inspector.

He admires the polished wood of the pistol's handle and the cold softness of the trigger despite it being made of steel.

So cold, the room. The woman is still whimpering, shaking her head in a violent 'No, no'.

Buva places the gun on the bed and pulls out the currency-note gag from her mouth. When he unties her hands, she slaps him, gently, still weeping.

He almost wants to put his arms around her to protect her from further harm.

The currency notes he has pulled out of her mouth fly around the room caught in the air-conditioner's draughts; one goes and sticks to the wet penis of Curly Head.

The woman pulls money out from the unconscious man's wallet, shoves a clutch of uncounted rupees in Buva's palm, turns him around and makes him face the door.

'Take your money, sorry, go. This is my job. Go. Don't get involved. Go!'

This is my job. This is my job.

You failed to identify a whore.

Buva, what's the matter with you?

You getting soft in your old age?

When he sits in the cab in shock, he leans his head against the steering wheel. Three-colour-rubber nipples on the cover of the wheel press an uncertain tattoo on his forehead.

So, okay, what if I made a mistake despite so many years of human watching?

Maybe she needs help. Will you abandon her because she flung a few hundred rupees extra in your face... and you accepted them?

Buva draws up his windows, leaving just enough space for air to get into the interior of Kamandalu, pulls out his key and walks towards the famous restaurant Kailash Parbat for his lunch.

He orders but does not enjoy the classic chhole bhature: the confusion in his gut battles the oil-rich food.

He returns to Kamandalu and opens the miniature version of the *Dasbodh*, looking for inspiration.

'The ability to decide what is kaarya, and what is akaarya, what is worth doing and what is not, is a quality of a pure person.'

He loses the battle against the stress of the decision.

He reaches for his tobacco pouch and his preferred brand of lime, Cow.

He meticulously picks and flings away the larger pieces of the leaf, leaving a miniature hill of even-sized tobacco in his palm, and then scoops the lime from the silver pod with his thumbnail and grinds it into the tobacco. He places the bolus between his lower gum and lip, waiting for the brown juice to reach his brain and open the faucets of adrenalin.

Someone taps on the window.

It's the woman from the flat, her head covered with a blood red scarf, eyes blanked out by wrap-around sunglasses, shirt smoothened, a cut on the upper lip.

He drops the meter even though there is no need to.

Her sunglasses become a magic lantern. Colaba Causeway, which ended the watery isolation of the island of Colaba from the rest of the Bombay in the 19th century, parades its glossy brand windows like a movie on the opaque black of her glasses; the names start squeezed, grow bulbous, then get squeezed again.

'Thank you.' Her voice is hoarse.

No, not for those two words, I did it for myself. I march to my manifesto, not yours.

The next time she is about to speak, they are on Marine Drive, and for a moment, the breeze catches her scarf unawares, threatening to smear blood on the pristine sky, a semaphore for air-conditioned violence.

Distracted, she grabs the scarf and wraps it around herself, battening down the shutters on her mystery.

Buva tries to return the extra money when she gets off

at Worli Naka, so close to his own residence; she refuses the offer with a shake of her head.

She walks off, carrying a heavy rucksack on her right shoulder and her purse on her left.

She trails a smell that is new, but before he can even think about it, two burly men in starched white lean down to catch his eye; one of them extends his arm and holds a crumpled chit of paper: Patthe Bapurao Marg.

'Know?'

'Know?'

He nods and then, under his impassive face, starts grinning inwardly.

I know everything there is to know about Mumbai.

Want to have a baby cobra bite your tongue and give you a high that will have you grinning for ten straight hours in a comatose sleep? Come with me to Darukhana.

Want to buy the world's finest hashish, the Malana variety from Himachal Pradesh, from a height of five thousand feet and selling in New York at one thousand dollars a pound? Come with me to Antop Hill, right under the noses of all three gods, Dargah Hajrat Shaikh, Antop Church and Gurdwara Sahib Singh.

Want to buy guns? Come with me to Tilak Nagar. Want to bet on matka? Come with me anywhere!

Patthe Bapurao Marg is the official name for Pila House,

recommended to these two out-of-towners by someone else who has tasted the morsels of flesh of the ageing whores, wearing pink and green nylon blouses, plastic butterflies pinned to a crumbling landscape.

So while the battered-blue woman returns home to nurse her wounds, these two romantics wander into the yellow chawls of the lane to look for someone like her, perhaps cheaper, and less accomplished.

The pimps pounce on them as soon as they step out of Kamandalu at Patthe Bapurao Marg.

Easy protein wrapped in identifiable starched khadi envelope straight from the hinterland.

The rest of the day is forgettable: it involves a continuous battle with the traffic signals, cab drivers who insist on travelling in the right lane, and youngsters riding their bikes like maniacs.

Buva returns to his hole in the BDD chawls, British Development Directorate's idea of housing for the lower middle classes, and waits for sunset.

A soundless shape arrives through the window, and jumps next to him. His tomcat partner, Kalya, black like him, but with green eyes and a purr-generating engine in his throat. Buva feeds him one large fish that he has bought on his way in, and then, after Kalya has finished his postprandial bath, they both settle down in the darkness.

Buva likes Kalya more than he likes most human beings.

He is very similar to me: black, alone, not worried about those around him, self-contained, content with his fate.

Of course, as we all know, life rarely leaves you alone.

Buva lights the oil lamp in front of Swami's photograph and crosses his legs to meditate. Just as he ferries human beings from one Mumbai to another during the day, he ferries himself to another place unsullied by the gloom of the chawl, deep within himself, at night.

Having finished his meditation, Buva slips into kurmaasan, the tortoise pose in yoga that allows one to behave like one.

Buva lies with his arms tucked under his legs spread wide, his chin touching the floor, as Kalya sits on his back, eyes closed.

Both withdraw the tentacles of their senses and retreat into a bubble of silence.

Two

_____

Madam Jeejebhoy and the Magic of Perfumes

Madam Jeroo Jeejebhoy of Malabar Hill used to travel with Buva daily for three years. She liked his clockwork precision, and she was the one who tutored him in perfumes, her favourite being Chanel No. 5.

He remembered the first time Madam Jeejebhoy got into his cab near Babulnath. She was speaking to herself loudly. 'How did I make this mistake, half an hour, now what happens to the flight, half an hour?'

She kept touching her thick spectacles nervously.

Buva had nodded a question in her direction, and she had explained in her accented Hindi.

She needed to reach the airport within fifty-five minutes because she had misread the flight timing.

'No problem.' Buva knew that phrase. And this was before the Sea Link had been inaugurated.

Buva knows that the total time spent at the traffic signals on the way to the airport is twenty-seven minutes; if he cut it down by half, he would deliver. Not waiting at signals—that was the key factor. Not waiting at signals without breaking traffic rules: that takes genius in Mumbai.

At fifty percent of the signals, he creates his own clover-leaf pattern by turning into left lanes, taking U-turns and then turning left again.

When they finally reach the airport, Jeroo Madam has a full eleven minutes in hand.

'Can you come at 9 a.m. every day to my house?'

From then on, she never said 'fast' or 'slow'; she just said, '10.30, Buva, 10.30 I have to be in Vikhroli, at the factory gate.'

She was the only woman, no, the only person, ever to deign to sit in the front seat with him.

Was it only because she wore an artificial foot?

'It's called Jaipur Foot, Buva, because Jaipur is the city

where it was invented,' she had offered the information as she twisted the meter's neck.

She knew about the whole world, and Buva loved her stories: she could talk about carrom, cabs, or perfumes.

'I don't know about India, Buva, but in Australia, the cab driver would get angry if I sat at the back... and anyway neither your cab nor you have an unpleasant smell... you must be using chandan, sandalwood, kem?'

'Buva, you know, even in Morocco, which is an Islamic country, single women sit in the front seat, with the driver, and talk... not like here... here they look down upon you, kem?'

Her laughter was always light, as if held afloat by a wave of cedar.

'Buva, you are the first Leftist taxi driver in Mumbai,' she said in her broken Hindi and laughed.

She struggled to explain the pun on Leftist, and Rightist, but Buva struggled to understand the concepts; he preferred material available to his senses.

All other cab drivers usurped the right lane, just so they could abandon their responsibility of looking in their rear-view mirrors.

'Buva, there is something called the New York moment... which is the time between the light turning green and the New York cabbie honking... thank god you don't like honking.' She laughed again.

Buva respected her most for her total disregard of public opinion. That's what Swami Samarth Ramdas had taught him too. He had learnt in his village and in BDD chawls the many ways in which human beings poured the acid of contempt on those dissimilar to themselves.

One Sunday morning in winter, he drove to a hundred-year-old Shah restaurant at Thakurdwar, meter at half-mast to indicate that he wasn't picking up fare, and bought the finest undhiyo ever made in Mumbai.

Eight layers of freshly cut vegetables and grapes had been stewed for hours in their own juices with ghee in a mud pot in an underground fire. When you opened the earthen lid, the fragrance of the mix swirled out, warming up the hardened edges of the cold in the air.

When the security guard refused to let him get into Jeroo Madam's building at Walkeshwar, he called her on her flat's intercom. She almost strangled the guard when she understood the reason for the discrimination. The denizens of one India always love to look down upon their brethren, snapping on a holier-than-the-English-speaker attitude as soon as it's convenient.

Her flat was a chaos of smells: flagons of coloured liquids swallowed the cold, hard light that bounced off the Arabian Sea's glittery carapace, and in the intervening semi-darkness, both her parents wandered around on wheelchairs.

He stood there, on the threshold, holding his earthen bowl of offering to the Goddess of Fragrance in his life.

'They don't remember my name any longer,' she told him.

Her parents are gazing at the horizon through the large windows, where the past could have been, where Bordi could have been.

He watches her feed the undhiyo to her parents.

It was like feeding small mechanical maws.

When she saw him staring at the coloured liquids, she explained what she did for a living.

'See, Buva, two plus two equals four in mathematics or yellow plus blue equals green in colour. But in perfumes? No. Everything is magical in perfumes.'

'You wear sandalwood, kem? Mix sandalwood and cedar... you must get woody perfume... but no... see, something much sweeter?'

Three

Young Buva and
the Lost Ant

B uva sat cross-legged in a picture-perfect village of
Khairlanji in interior Maharashtra, in Bhandara
district, just at the edge of the neighbouring state
of Madhya Pradesh. Smoke drifted out of some huts, but
you can't see it because it is late night, though you can smell
its acrid cow dung insistence.

He lay snuffling, a confused eight-year-old, not
wanting to get his hot-headed father angry at the end of
a tiring day.

His mom sat next to him, engulfing her sole child in a cloud of familiar smells.

He had adored her. He remembered the beautiful tattoo on her chin like a blue rangoli on a brown earth background. He remembered the smell of milk and the leather that she cured all day and the ash she used to clean her hands with.

'What happened?' she whispered.

'The ant.'

'What ant?'

'She came into our house... on my shorts...when I was playing...'

'Arre, Naru, ants go everywhere...'

'But now she is away from her friends and brothers and sisters and parents... How will she find them again?'

'God looks after everybody....'

'Don't teach him rubbish,' his father hisses from the corner, where he is attempting to read in the light of the fire.

'Naru, ants know how to find their way home.'

It terrifies him—the distance between his hut and the place where he was playing. The poor lost ant. Without food. Without water. Without friends.

He imagines himself like the ant, not knowing that he will be like her one day.

The ant may not experience sorrow, may not have a

memory of a lost sisterhood, may depend only on chemical crumbs to find her way back to her colony. (How long does an ant last without food anyway?)

How do human beings return home?

Four

Pakya and Self-Respect

P oliomyelitis is not an egalitarian disease. It victimises no living species except homo sapiens.

But Pakya never asked why he was chosen by the Russian roulette of destiny, or why the asymmetrical paralysis got his arm rather than leg.

Pakya uses his left hand as if he has no right. The policeman who accosted him for the Left Hand Drive board on his bicycle was dumbstruck by his reply: 'I use only my left hand to ride, so Left Hand Drive... what's wrong?'

As if to compensate for this handicap, Pakya has multiple

skills: he has been blessed with sensory organs like giant vacuum cleaners.

He sucks in higher gigabytes of information than most human beings. Just as the housefly's iridescent compound eyes can watch your swatter coming towards it in laughably slow motion, Pakya has learnt to process the information and anticipate the future.

In his adolescence, he had been party to the flesh-tearing raids that the gangs of BDD chawls mounted on other gangs, but soon he had filtered in enough street-smartness to choose sides. Pakya drifted to the side of the law, not because it was right, but because it was more convenient.

The carrom is his playground, since the game of cricket is out of bounds for him.

Here, on the three feet by three feet smooth plywood, his striker nudges, pushes, kicks, and plunges into corner abysses wooden circles of red, white and black.

During the day, he does the same with information, nudging tidbits into the waiting ears of hairy policemen— information gathered while trawling through the bars and taxi stands.

The Mumbai Police have a separate secret-service fund for khabris: guys who have opted out of gangs or are still looking for revenge. Some of them exchange dead-ends and fake news, but the police don't mind filtering the data since it comes from a network distributed across the six-hundred-odd square kilometres of Mumbai.

Pakya's first memory is of mud, his attempt to crush it within his aching fingers in uncontrolled anger, as he watches *Deewar*, the Hindi film that established Amitabh Bachchan aka Lambu as the voice of the oppressed. The crowd sits in the courtyards between the huge chawls, watching the film from both sides of the screen.

Pakya sits on the platform built around one of the restless ficuses, and an inquisitive shrew bites into his bulbous toe. Pakya jerks it off absent-mindedly, as his spirit gets sucked by a six-foot tall man with a deep voice taking on a gang of paid hoodlums.

'Main aaj bhi pheke hue paise nahin uthaata.'

'Don't fling money at me; hand it over with respect,' says Amitabh Bachchan's character Vijay, despite being a lowly shoeshine boy.

Self-respect or death, that's the way to live.

Anger as a weapon of self-redemption.

That's why Pakya leads the charge against anybody when they act uppity.

What is a dada? A gangster boss?

The BDD chawls have their own lessons on the subject.

A man who doesn't care about the future.

To whom violence is a lance that cuts open suppurating boils inside his own mind.

Bhenchod, what else is there to live for? Look at my dad, licking the boots of the mill owners even after they had kicked him in the balls and asked him to leave.

Pakya's dad has been one of the one-and-a-half lakh victims of the cotton mill strikes in 1981. It was Pakya's resourcefulness in providing information to gangs about police movement that kept the family fed.

But Pakya's anger against the world has no taproot-sucking toxicity.

Unlike the Brahmins in Khairlanji, who hated the idea of young Buva getting into school, Pakya's blood is not charred.

Pakya just doesn't like anybody opposing him.

Buva and Pakya were adolescents hunting in Hanuman Lane near Sadhana Cinema.

The women came out at night after eight o'clock, dressed in flashy sarees and bright lipstick, some twirling their plaits intertwined with bright ribbons, some whistling, some chewing paan.

Buva and Pakya were hunting for mates, their primal brains sparked off by colour and voice and shape, everything on the outside; they will have to wait for a long time to experience the act of falling in love.

Buva and he, they had both stood near Reshma, since they were told that she was new. That was twenty years ago.

They stood squabbling near Reshma, and the madam had walked out and told them in her uncharacteristically soft voice not to create a nuisance, and better for BDD chawl guys to settle their fights in BDD chawls rather than in her beautifully painted bedrooms.

The fight lasted two minutes.

Buva did not want to hurt Pakya because of his disability but had underestimated his street-level cunning when he pulled out a knife and slashed at him, missing Buva's stomach and instead ripping his thigh.

That was the only chance Pakya got. When Buva hit him on his nose with a hammerhead of a fist, he had blacked out.

That was also the last time they were on the opposing sides of a dividing line.

Five

Young Buva and the Raining Rocks

J ust outside the window, a bottle filled with kerosene and lit by a wick lands, crashes and bursts into flames, announcing the beginning of yet another caste war.

It's 1972.

Thirteen-year-old Buva wakes up from his dreams to the worst caste riots in the history of BDD chawls and Bombay.

He cowers in the corner of the mori, reducing the size of his body to reduce injury, while his uncle stands outside the door with a knife, waiting for attacks he too can't believe would happen in a city like Bombay.

The police vans arrive an hour later. But they are ill-equipped to deal with the ingenious resistance from both factions, the lower castes and the upper.

When the police van parks next to a building, they have not reckoned with the preparations made by the angry mobs.

They have carried ten- and twenty-kilo rocks to the roofs of the chawls.

They refuse to accept state intervention for matters deeply woven with personal identity.

The riots are unprecedented, even for the old BDD folks: they have never witnessed twenty thousand Dalits emerging from the by lanes, disarming the police with their sheer numbers, and worse, preparedness.

When the unsuspecting police vans enter the tiled lanes within the chawls, they are crippled by the huge rocks flung from the roofs.

The police are unable to respond quickly: when the rocks have hit the engines, no progress is possible. The team just gets out and runs for safety.

The vans that have their engines intact rush out in panic, in turn blocking traffic between chawls and at the outlets that lead to the main road.

The suppressed anger of the 'Untouchable Dalits', captured by the novelist Namdeo Dhasal and speaker Raja Dhale finds a steely new expression in the chawls.

Only the police own firearms, even if they are antiquated .303 rifles, and most damage is caused by fire, steel and stone.

The chosen weapons include the famed nine- to twelve-inch gravity knife, the classical Rampuri, named after its genesis in Rampur in Uttar Pradesh, light bulbs filled with acid, tube lights, bicycle chains and stones.

Buva is yet to be named Buva by the chawls. His uncle still calls him Narayan or Naru, and as he scrunches his eyes and covers his ears to shut out the sounds of rage and bloodshed, he remembers what his father had told him and why he had given him the *Dasbodh*.

Apparently, Swami Ramdas had met the Sikh Guru Hargobind, and asked him, 'Why do you call yourself a saint when you carry a sword?'

The Sikh guru had replied, 'I am a saint inside me, but I will not tolerate oppression of the weak by the mighty... outside me.'

And that is how Swami Ramdas started his social revolution: equality of gender and equality of caste, fighting fire with fire.

Naru becomes Buva within himself, as he resolves to

become strong enough to fight for his self-esteem. No more quaking in fear.

As the violence spirals out of control, the police open fire.

Eleven Dalits are killed in 1972.

Nine more than in Buva's village Khairlanji, in Bhandara.

The BDD chawls will continue to be an arena for multiple riots, fuelled by the remorseless pursuit of power by gang lord Dawood Ibrahim and his rivals.

BDD, the amphitheatre of arson and assassination is where the ruthless puppet masters play youngsters against each other, watching the bloodshed from the sidelines, from the rarity of air-conditioned rooms, rooms turned grey from the smoke of 555 cigarettes and fumes of Johnny Walker whisky.

Buva is never involved.

Six

Young Sylvia and the Hoopoe of Vasai

I t was not clear to twenty-six-year-old Sylvia how exactly her husband Vernon died.

She had known him since school, in Vasai. They both belonged to the Anglo-Indian community, the Chrysalis community, waiting to burst onto the Indian ecosystem as possible butterflies, carrying the twin DNAs of Indians and the English.

She had stood in the shadows when the adolescent mating rituals had begun. All the bright clothes, exaggerated hand waving, and the self-conscious tittering made her want to melt into the background.

Sylvia was called the Shrinking Violet by her school and college mates, the shyness probably a result of losing her parents unexpectedly during her childhood.

But she had fallen in love with Vernon, who rarely postured and whistled at girls. She had fallen in love because he danced so well. Vernon rarely spoke; he let his body do the talking—at the community balls, at the stolen teenage night-outs, in the school playground, even when he was practising when he thought nobody was looking.

His legs twirled between his arms when he was on the floor. His legs went above his head and he sprung up like a Jack in the Box toy her father had given her. Grace coiled around strength, as one movement rivered into another.

It was the community's monthly visit to the Vasai Fort— the ruins that had inspired many Hindi film-song shoots portraying lovelorn youngsters framed by arched stone. The strange upside down baobab tree stood at the seaside, its roots sucking the sky. A hoopoe walked in the grass, nodding Yes and Yes as he picked up insects, his sharp black-and-white crown slicing the briny air into bits.

Sylvia was lost in her own world, in an uncertain future, defined by the horizon she could see from the fort.

The stones had stood the onslaught of the waves since

the 12th century. How can two contradictions coexist? Something so strong and unmoving, something so strong and always moving. Stone and sea.

His shadow snapped her out of her reverie.

'Can I watch what you are watching?'

She smiled.

'You can't hide, you know, Sylvia… I know you watch me.'

'I'll invent a dance for you… we will call it Sylventine,' he had whispered, smiling through his moustache.

She doesn't know where the courage comes from.

'What do I have to do… to watch you do the Sylventine?'

'It can't be done.'

'What do you mean… you just said…?'

'My Sylventine can't be done alone.'

He ends her confusion.

'You will have to marry me.'

Will the sea find stone?

Something, or someone, tangible to hold on to during a continental drift of uncertainty.

She knew he worked for Stanley, who was a big shot on the seas of Mumbai, from Sassoon Dock and its fishermen and fisherwoman community to Apollo Bunder and its hip South Mumbai set.

The first needed good old-fashioned alcohol in multiple

forms, naringi and beer and McDowell's No. 1 'quarters' and single malts from Speyside and Japan and the second needed new-age chemicals: angel dust, cocaine, heroin, amyl nitrite.

Thankfully, Vernon had remained a teetotaller, a vow he had made when he watched his alcoholic father and brother sliding down the painful, slippery slope, screaming as they hallucinated about snakes sinking their fangs into their testicles, about rabid dogs snarling in the dark around their beds, about their shirts catching fire.

But without being conscious of it, she got addicted to the other thing that Vernon did well: make love. His stamina in bed matched his stamina on the dance floor. He broke down her barriers, one body curve at a time, explained to her how women must enjoy their bodies as men do, no sin in that, no need to listen to what the pastor said; after all, it was between husband and wife. It was nobody else's concern.

He set alight every cell, every pleasure spot she did not know existed. The arch of the neck, the gentle valley around the navel, the insides of her thighs, the soles of her feet, the web between her fingers—his tongue tattooed out a Morse code of pleasure as intense as pain.

Vernon played her body like an instrument until she exploded, toes curling, a warm crimson tide in her brain drowning out all thought.

The shrinking violet turned into a blooming rose, and

the bed became an opera that celebrated symphonies of the skin.

Dear Lord, give us this day our daily fuck.

She adored him.

He needed to spend several nights away, and she had been displaced from Vasai to Mahim, in a small fisherfolk community, and yet, she used the memories of their moments together as a warm blanket.

After so many years out on a sea of unknowing, she had an anchor.

She smiles more, and more often, and the children bask in her smothering attention.

He loved their children to distraction, son and daughter, a perfect pair. Every time he returned from a trip on the seas, there were always three gifts: one for her, and one each for the boy and the girl. Star-spangled ribbons and talking dolls for the daughter, a battery-powered Patton tank for the son, and an incredibly exotic burgundy lipstick for her that made her lips look wet like washed cherries.

When he wasn't travelling, they enjoyed trips that middle-class India had no access to, because these were trips by sea and by speedboats provided by Stanley, his boss and benefactor. They went from Mahim to a quiet beach house in Mandwa, or to his friend's house in Elephanta Caves (no electricity, so the opera on the bed played longer), or to a seaside cottage in Uran, all via the Gateway of India in less than forty minutes.

And then suddenly, like a monstrous hairy hand ripping out a page in a fairy-tale book that is six happy years long, came that phone call at the crack of dawn, as the sun nudged the horizon awake at Colaba, the centre of Vernon and Stanley's lives.

It was a gravelly voice. 'I'm Stanley. Vernon worked with me. Come quickly to the Saint George's Hospital; it is next to VT station. Take a taxi. Quickly.'

She had asked her neighbour to keep an eye on her sleeping babies, just five- and four-year-old darlings, and jumped into a cab at the edge of the lane in Mahim.

The hospital has announced him DOA.

What does that mean, she asked the nurse, ashen faced.

'Madam, it is "dead on arrival". What to do…hospital, no, couldn't help him.'

I have no mother, no father, no brother, now no Vernon.

Stanley puts an arm around her shoulder; his demeanour does not match his gruff voice.

Curly hair, curly beard, bloodshot eyes.

'I'm sorry; he fell over while he was drunk.'

But he never drinks. He is a teetotaller; his father died— can't be.

'That's what the postmortem says.'

'No,' she screams.

'Shh, shh, look, Sylvia, I will look after everything, you go back, go back… go to your children in my car. George, take her. I will call when we are ready with the funeral.'

She reaches home and vomits in terror as she weeps.

The Vasai Fort stone has crumbled; the sea enters her nostrils, her lungs, her brain.

Seven

Young Shalini and Petrichor

'Buvaaa, Buvaaa, Buvaaa.'

Buva is wrenched out of his sleep by a thin, adolescent voice.

It's still dark outside, and he can smell the fragrance of the rain, as their fierce globules kick geosmins out of the dust.

Kalya yawns on his chest, advertising his spectacular canines, and then jumps off.

The voice belongs to Shalini, the fifteen-year-old girl who sells lemon juice at Worli to help herself get through night school. It was Buva who had come up with the idea for her and negotiated space on the footpath with the local municipal thug-in-charge. She would stand behind a stainless-steel vessel covered with a wet red cloth, placed on a bed of ice and lemons, and sell a glassful to Mumbaiites crossing over to the Worli Sea Face promenade.

Education is the door to the other India, he'd explained to Shalini. You must study hard.

He splashes water on his face in the mori in the corner and bows to Swami's image. When he opens the door, Shalini starts sobbing.

'Buva, Baba is not home... yesterday also...'

She has had her body stared at ever since she developed bumps on her chest, this little girl with twin braids of hair framing her round face. She is wary of physical contact in this city of transactions, so she holds herself back even though she trusts Buva unconditionally, fists knotted to prevent the panic from slipping out of her hands.

He senses her discomfort, curbs his own instinct to console her, steps out with his keys and a torch and strides down the corridor, a stone morgue for snoring bodies.

There's Kannan Nair, the Malayali giant who flings heavy bags in Mumbai's ancient docks all day, who flopped dead tired, every muscle soaking the relaxing hardness of the floor.

Sukku Nair, his twin, a bouncer at the Ghetto Club, has just returned from work and gone to sleep. If you needed cocaine, he'd try to get it for you from the wannabes of the entertainment industry who create their desi headbangers' ball every day.

Then there's Mahesh, the pillar at Vichare Couriers, Mumbai's local courier service, who pounds the pavements from morning to dusk.

The females of the family sleep within the rooms, but most of the doors are open, unlike in the Eye Nation.

Thankfully, unlike most other BDD chawls, Buva's chawl has separate toilets for men and women, allowing a greater sense of privacy.

Of course, if your olfactory bulb is well developed, you will sense that all the pillows are coated with the residue of hair oil, deepened by jasmine or rose or amla, its application a practice that the rich Mumbai has abandoned in favour of expensive minoxidil and finasteride.

Buva is looking for a specific brother-in-arms for his rescue mission.

When he finally finds him, the snoring man is lying with his mouth open as if eager to swallow all that the dreams of the future offer him. His right arm, a bony stump, covers only his right eye. Buva pulls off the checkered sheet and applies the cool touch of his still-wet fingers to his eyelids;

it's a shame demolishing the fragrant-filigreed structure of any dream.

'Pakya, Pakya, chal, let's go.'

His whisper is a plea.

Pakya has morphed from competitor to friend to partner in Buva's life. He yawns, scratches his armpit with boric-acid-stained fingers of his healthy left arm, and curls back into his sheet.

'Pakya, let's go.'

Pakya is also the most tenacious competitor on the carrom board, and sometimes practices by himself till late into the night, half his face illumined by the low bulb that both lights the carrom board and warms it to fight Mumbai's soupy humidity.

'Buva, make no mistake, carrom is not just a local game, it's an international game. They play in Germany, America, many places,' Madam Jeejebhoy had mentioned once.

The three of them bundle into Kamandalu. Shalini sits behind, sniffling. Pakya is wearing his short-sleeved banyan, his head still weighed down by sleep, next to Buva.

Kamandalu moves.

'Where?'

Pakya jerks his head up. He stares around, and then mumbles.

'Moti... Moti Talkies.'

The area is a rainforest of concrete, populated with fluorescent, synthetic sari-clad prostitutes, taciturn sellers of boiled eggs and boiled gram, attendees of a Sai Baba pooja, drunkards snuffling the dirt of the footpaths wrapped around a tree or streetlight pole, all dissolved into running streaks of colour and light on the windscreen lashed by rain. Pakya rubs his eyes, gets off and walks along the trundling cab, peering at the bodies.

It's on his second round up the street that he signals to Buva.

Shalini rushes out the moment Buva brakes.

One-armed Pakya and Shalini drag her father Ganesh to the cab, propping him up on their shoulders. They shove him in the back seat, and Shalini somehow manages to squeeze herself next to the stinking body of her progenitor. Pakya resumes his seat next to Buva, who is guiltily happy he opted for washable rexine seats instead of cloth.

It is when they reach out of the lane that Shalini starts screaming.

Three hours later, Buva stands with his head hanging over the flowered and garlanded corpse of Shalini's father. Ganesh lies cold, cotton balls in his nostrils, tulasi leaves between his lips, another human life tracing an incomprehensible trajectory of self-destruction.

Most of those standing around the corpse are employees who can afford to be off work in state government and municipal organisations. Those in the private industry have hurriedly placed stringy garlands, touched Ganesh's claw-like feet and left to mark their presence on long registers in their offices.

Shalini has crumbled; she holds Buva around his waist and sobs uncontrollably. Despite himself, he can feel tears prick his eyes. But his tears won't fall. He stopped weeping and laughing many years ago, in a village that was more cruel than the city, in a village that sifted human beings into superior and inferior.

'Death is time's truncheon… it bothers not whether you are a villain, a warrior, wealthy man or ascetic,' says the *Dasbodh*.

Why do you weep, Shalini, why? What did he give you as a father?

He gave you the name Shalini, meaning the 'modest one', and then did everything to destroy your modesty.

Buva remembers another rainy night, rushing to their tiny room and holding back a flailing, angry Ganesh, saving a trembling ball in the corner, Shalini, from being violated by her own father.

When you are an HIV patient, you cling on to any piece of advice from any quack, and the oldest nostrum devised by the insensitive patriarchal bastards to cure yourself of the virus was to have sex with a virgin.

What cheaper, more convenient victim than your own daughter?

Buva had requested Sushitai, the widow nurse who stayed two rooms away, to allow Shalini to sleep in her room at night. Now, of course, Shalini would be able to return to her own room. Perhaps she would have to live behind closed doors.

When he starts Kamandalu that afternoon, after the cremation at Charni Road and after a bath, his eyes are heavy from lack of sleep.

The smell of burning flesh has unwrapped something, but Buva doesn't know it.

Eight

Buva and the Playwright

I am getting old. I can't take punishment. Just one sleepless night is taking its toll.

The early rain has steamed up the city. The dust has turned into a thin, slippery skin on the tar, and Buva watches several self-absorbed youngsters on two-wheelers get into uncontrollable skids, their egos bruised as much as their unprotected bums covered in expensive polyester.

Buva has his own label for them: Non-Pass Boys. They just couldn't take life's exams well.

Buva invents words that join the two cities of English and non-English.

To him, the self-conscious girl is an 'aarsa addict' (mirror addict); the mobile phone whisperer is 'teen kaani' (three-eared).

Smells have no names, so he entertains Jeroo Jeejebhoy with names he has invented, words that are onomatopoeic.

The smell of Dadar market early in the morning is 'pudigreen', a portmanteau of pudina and green, locking within its 'p' and 'n' the fresh affront of crushed mint and a host of other vegetables with their juices extracted by thousands of trampling human feet and the squishing of giant tyres of the municipality dumper that comes to clear the debris.

The smell of Dharavi is 'gardili', the expiration of a dense crowd's labour and the gossamer liliness of their touching dreams.

She laughs when he says Malabar Hill is 'jejunum', telling him that the word has meaning in English itself, and perhaps he is right in calling that neighbourhood barren in its approach to the rest of Mumbai.

He thinks of Madam Jeejebhoy as he drives himself to his private resting place—the road along Worli Sea Face.

Love knows neither temperature nor humidity: couples hug each other sitting on Worli Sea Face promenade's low wall that is getting ready to face the slaphappy monsoon waves despite the thirty-three-degree temperature and ninety-degree humidity.

Another sea rises within the couples, yearning for union and dissolution both.

Buva's head rests against his favourite multicoloured beaded steering wheel, and he feels the tug as the sea is sucked out. It always happens when that secret smell escapes the tightly screwed vials of memory—the smell of burning flesh.

'Chalenge?'

There is a khaki-clad youngster, smelling of half-wet clothes, peering through the window, one presumptuous hand on the meter.

He is taken aback by Buva's bloodshot eyes, but Buva nods Yes.

The youngster wrings the meter's neck, sits in front but unconsciously shrinks closer to the door.

They reach a building on the opposite side of the road, and while Buva wonders why anybody would not merely cross the street, he realises the khaki-clad security guard is helping an old couple reach the cancer hospital in Parel.

The old woman's fair, shiny skin is set off by a deep orange sari and blouse, and the partition in her oiled white hair is an exclamation mark ending in a large red bindi on her forehead. She is supporting her partner, attempting to hold him upright. He is clean-shaven, wears an old-fashioned black topi, and stares at the cab vacantly. Flesh hangs on his facial bones as if put out to dry.

Buva steps out hurriedly and opens the door. The man slides in, exhausted by the walk; the woman gets in through the other door.

Top note of naphthalene balls, middle note of ghee, bottom note of proud surrender.

'What time do you want to reach?' He looks at the woman in the rear-view mirror, with his standard first question.

She smiles. 'We have overstayed our welcome anyway, my son. Take your time.'

Looks very different from my earth-tinted mother, but the same acceptance of the river of life.

'Son abroad?'

She smiles, rather than get irritated by his nosiness.

'Arre waah... a driver with siddhis... extrasensory powers... can look at the past... can tell our future too, then?'

It is Buva's turn to smile sheepishly.

'Sorry.'

'It's written, no...?' She indicates the lines of fate on the forehead.

'Swami Samarth says, we can live on in our fame, keerti, even after—'

Both the woman and Buva are startled by the man's explosive laugh.

He laughs till he coughs, bending over, growing red in his face, as tears flow down his cheeks. At the traffic signal, Buva turns, looks at him and places his palm on the hand clutching the front seat.

The woman sighs, and thumps her husband's back.

'He hates depending on others. He was a famous writer of Marathi plays. Our son...'

The man whispers to her, pointing to Buva.

'He says he knows the shloka you are referring to... written by Ramdas Buva... he is not afraid of dying, just fed up of going to the hospital so many times.'

Deep inside Buva, another faint memory rises. This man. The same year that the 1972 riots happened between the upper castes and the Dalits, this man had been criticised for being a Brahmin who wrote against Brahmins.

He is hesitant, but his curiosity gets the better of him.

'Mai, is he the famous playwright? Is he Ramesh Joshi?'

She nods.

He had written a play that mocked the Brahmins of Pune for exploiting the lower castes.

Who is the enemy, then, if Brahmins fight Brahmins, backward castes fight backward castes?

Kamandalu takes them from the sunnier, posher, Arabian Sea-welcoming Western Mumbai to Central Mumbai, the womb of an older industrial Mumbai, all old stone bridges and mill buildings, dense, congested, unexposed to the soothing breeze of the sea, compacted desires and angry youngsters exploding in political parties that milk their naïveté, where real-estate czars in dance bars plot the exchange of land for lucre.

Right in the middle of it all, defying the grubbiness, a monument to Parsi generosity, is the Tata Cancer Hospital, one of the finest in the world, yet dispensing advice and medicine free of cost.

As the couple gets off, Buva offers to help them negotiate the corridors, but the woman refuses.

Buva parks the cab, rolls up the windows, locks up and walks briskly back to the corridors of the hospital.

The woman sighs in relief as Buva's iron arms hold the man and takes the weight off her shoulders. He leans towards Buva; his mouth puffs out sharp notes of the cardamom he is chewing.

'There are many kinds of cancer. My son suffers from the type that transforms heart muscle into stone.' His whisper again ends in laughter, and a cough that moves the cage of ribs inside him violently.

His wife shakes her head, indulgent in her disbelief.

The trio enters a cavern of carbolic acid mixed with putrid tissue.

They should make hospitals in meadows, with marigold yellow flowers and iridescent birds flying in bright sunshine, making you feel happy to be alive rather than be afraid of dying,

Most of all, hospitals should smell nice, of life, of hope, of magnolias, sandalwood, kittens.

Ward 27. The entrance is guarded by two wooden benches where men and women sit propped against each other, switched off from the reality of an imminent death.

They gorge on what is available now, or go back to banquets in the past, finding mechanisms to deal with the inevitable.

'I hold tight my sari gifted many years ago by my daughter-in-law when she got her first paycheck, pinch tight the past between my two fingers. I am fortunate I was never despised by my family. I can go, leave, start to the other side.'

'When I was ten, I had been carried to a hospital at night in pouring rain by my dad because he suspected I had diptheria, and I refused to open my mouth for the night-duty doctor, and I wish I could refuse now too to stand and get many rays of poison into my bones.'

'My son will never return.... He thinks this cancer is my revenge on his successful career.'

'Shall I wait, Mai?' Buva asks the old woman.

She shakes her head again.

'Lots of time, we have lots of time....' Then she touches his shoulder and says quietly, 'Ayushman bhava.'

'Parva yeshil?'

'Will you come and fetch us the day after?' she asks Buva, offering him one new fixed customer, and one more rip in the fabric of the perfect life that Buva seeks.

Mrs and Mr Joshi, his second fixed income. Maybe he should not charge them anything for his service. Abandoned by a rich son, maybe a poor son can make up for the insult.

Looking for your mother, Buva, looking for your mother?

She jumped into a well lined by furious dry rocks, ha ha ha, as the others laughed... and so did your father die in that well when he leapt in to save her.

Buva chased her only to haplessly clutch at the strings of the stench of her burning flesh.

He bit the arms that held him back, an animal thrashing to survive, wanting to leap into the blackness after her.

Next evening, after both parents had been cremated, his mother's brother decided he didn't want to risk his innocence any further. He had to be packed off to Bombay because Bombay doesn't look beyond the colour of skin.

Or so he thought.

I want to bury my head in something and shut out the world that refuses to listen to Swami Samarth Ramdas.

I want to bury my head in Reshma's silken hair.

Nine

Reshma and the
Three-Letter Killer

The sight of Buva makes even the jaded eyes of the prostitutes spark up in surprise as they wash off the previous night's detritus stuck in the slits and crevices of their bodies.

They are sitting on their haunches, at the corners of the corridors, in flowery cotton nighties, the uniform of the lower- and middle-class Indians, gagging as they scrub their tongues, scrunching their eyes as they whip the wetness off their long hair, gargling away the taste of alien tongues and penises.

Buva has returned to Pila House after months or years; he has been struggling to stay away from Reshma, his Samarth Ramdas desire to remain unattached wrestling with his human desire to procreate.

Buva climbs slowly up to the third floor and reaches room 308.

Sunanda the madam is getting a massage, grunting in pleasure while chewing her paan expertly, a ruminant procurer of fresh flesh, slave driver and confidante of virgins. She is lying face down, her silk sari hitched up (Sunanda always wore silk saris), as her fat calves are pummelled by two young girls.

One of the youngsters automatically reaches out to ring the bell that will summon the girls who are ready to sit with their customers, but Sunanda has recognised Buva's black mirror-polished shoes.

She raises herself on her elbow, flicks her pallu back on to her shoulder, and emits a mix of sighs and groans. 'Buva... long time!'

She picks up her brass spittoon, and expertly unloads the remains of her paan.

'So many months... business is okay or what? Shifted to Andheri Vandheri?'

She gestures to one of the girls, thumb to lip, little finger askew, and the girl walks out into the corridor and whistles her order for tea, 'Three cutting.'

Sunanda knots her hair, but does not get up, which is very rare for her in front of a client.

'Sorry, Buva... my back is finished, Buva. I get up only once or twice a day... toot gayi... broken.'

Buva sits silent, holding tight all sense tendrils in his fists. Hold. Wait. Don't react. Wait. Hold. Listen to the moment, not to the past.

The sound of Sunanda chewing the remainder of her paan, two young girls giggling in the corridor, and a woman singing an aarti flood his ears.

'She is not here, Buva. Reshma is not here.'

She looks at her own feet, protruding, splay-toed, a counterpoint to the delicate gold geometry on her sari border.

She avoids looking at Buva as she speaks.

'I pay for her medicines; she was my lucky girl, everybody's friend, but this new disease has no friends... bekaar... samzhe na tum... you understand?'

Buva stands till the meaning of the words gently leaches into his brain; the words match the wall paintings by the National Aids Control Organisation.

'She may have it; you may not know it.'

He lowers himself down on the iron cot, coiled up and limp at the same time.

The two girls stare at him, one of them chewing gum, a calculated disinterest that may be attractive to this muscled bearded weirdo; the other is twirling half her oiled plait in the air, genuinely curious about Buva, his untimely arrival and his uneasy silence.

For Buva, everything in the known universe was in its place till a few hours ago.

The predictions of the Indian meteorological department and Indian calendar month, Aashad, seventy-eight years ahead of the Gregorian, were equally matched to welcome the monsoon.

The Bandra–Worli Sea Link was to open soon, making Kamandalu's access to the suburbs thirty minutes shorter.

CNG access points for taxis had tripled.

Then the whole canvas bled white and vanished and was replaced by violent frames.

A nervous young lady had turned out to be a prostitute who got paid for being tortured.

A famous playwright, who revolutionised theatre, abandoned by his mammon-obsessed son, had his bones hollowed by the maggots of cancer.

Ganesh, brain dissolved in alcohol, body under attack by an unfriendly virus, had slithered off the edge, leaving his already exposed daughter at the mercy of BDD chawls, and now, Reshma.

'Hospital? Which?' His deep voice is barely audible, strangled by emotions new to him.

He brushes aside the glass of tea offered to him.

'Buva, her full name is Seema Bishnu Chowdhury... because the hospital... they will ask you.'

Seema Bishnu Chowdhury, aka Reshma.

Sold by her parents in a small village in the Sunderbans for a princely sum of two thousand rupees when she was fourteen, having reached puberty, the oldest of seven children.

After a three-day journey with other unaffordable daughters in 4DN Howrah Mail, her games of hopscotch and climbing trees in search of fruit end, and she becomes a fleshy toy under hairy men, living away from their wives, unable to control their lust.

Seema.

In that endless blur of naked men to whom she was just an orifice, came a dark, quiet, shy youngster, who did everything slowly, and then later, bought her tiny gifts, mostly perfumes that she wore when she was with him.

She harboured no hopes of returning to Kolkata or of getting married and settling down, for those were beyond the reach of any of her friends: they had been fed stories of how some girls tried leaving against the wishes of Sunanda, and got abused by their new-found partners so steadily that they returned to the happy numbness of Pila House.

The SEM Hospital has a separate ward for HIV-afflicted patients.

Buva asks the ward boy whether he knows where Seema is.

Since the discovery of the disease in India in 1986 and the medical experts' brazen claims of having found a cure in 1993, thankfully, more misconceptions than patients have died here.

'That one from Pila House... bed 69.'

That waterfall of black silk on her head he adored has been replaced by a bald head with a few strands stuck to it with sweat. It takes time for the neural connections in Buva's brain to readjust to the image from the past.

'Buva?'

Her first word is a question; she is yet aware that her memory plays tricks, leads her astray. Her eyes are unable to focus.

'Buva!'

She appears to bloom; her smile grows wider displaying gums desperately holding on to decaying stubs of dentine.

Her memory brings back more and more morsels of caring that Buva had bestowed.

At their first meeting, Buva's mind was a wrestling match between his muscular twenty-year-old libido and his equally muscular guru's diktats.

His body was demanding sexual intercourse, but his mind was warning him against becoming a householder.

Four centuries ago, his guru had rushed out of his wedding ceremony, moments before the unsuspecting bride was to place the final bonding garland around his neck.

Reshma had been in business long enough to understand what the hesitant youngsters were looking for, and she had guided Buva gently, without creating cracks in the fragile innocence.

'Buva!'

He sits next to her, gently raises her till she is upright against the iron rods of the bed till she sighs and rests against his arm.

This white safari shirt is his second; its sleeves carry no wounds.

'Buva.'

'Still… that lovely sandalwood smell…'

'Shhh…'

'Buva… listen…'

'Shhh… rest… you are tired.'

A fan with an unhinged cup rotates furiously, attempting

to churn air heavy with smells of pus and antiseptic floor cleaners.

All hospitals smell the same, irrespective of the destinies of their patients.

Ayurvedic experts say tears of joy flow from the outer edges of the eye, of pain from the middle, and of regret from the inner corners.

She wipes her tears with her pallu and whispers.

'Buva... there was a third person... ours... tiny...' She holds the being in the cup of her hand, on her stomach.

Buva does not understand what she has said.

Just when she is about to repeat herself, he turns and faces her.

Her mouth smells rancid, gases released by cells going berserk.

'She was ours... yours, mine.'

'*Sansar tyag na karita, prapanch upadhi na sanditaa...*' whispers a muscular saint.

'No, my child, running away from normal life, and living the normal life, are both illusions.'

She had found some way of blocking others, and accepting him.

Or had she?

She was special, but she was a prostitute after all.

But why would she lie to him now?

Back and forth, truth or lies, life or death.

No, on the verge of death, with nothing to gain, she can't be telling a lie.

She had found a way to stop others, and accept him.

Two snakes of twisted nucleic molecules hugged each other in a warm, pulpy place and created a third person.

There must have been a tiny beating heart linked to Reshma's and his, asking for acceptance.

There must have been tiny fingers reaching out like they show on TV in the anti-abortion Doordarshan ads, asking unheard questions: 'Baba, am I a Dalit like you or a Hindu converted into a Muslim like Reshma?'

Madams who own prostitutes rarely monitor the pregnancy-prevention techniques of their slaves on a day-to-day basis.

Keep these basics in mind, you idiots, because the man grunting on top of you hasn't the slightest interest in what his sperm ends up as, so get that Copper-T inserted or better still get him a condom if he agrees.

Men are desperate to deposit their seed; you must be equally desperate to keep it out.

Ten

JJ and the Guava Tree

Olfaction is part of the subconscious.

It's the first sense that's activated when we're born. And it continues to remain active throughout our lives, because it contains the only neurons in the body that get replaced every month.

In Bordi in Gujarat, in the navel of Parsi culture, time is arthritic.

It hobbles along between the casuarina trees, occasionally casting glances at the horizon through cataracted eyes. It rests with a sigh on the creaky, brotherly swing in the porch, lung sacks made heavy with the smell of the chikoo fruit.

But Jeroo and her brother Vispy love the guava tree in the courtyard. Guava wood is the most resilient, so Vispy can hang upside down on slender branches and they won't betray his trust. Jeroo is fourteen and has many strange sensations when she lies on a branch between her legs. She makes the branch move up and down, up and down.

Let me go up away from Vispy so he does not see how much I enjoy it. The sun is a blanket soaked in the sea moisture. Up and over, Jeroo, where your brother cannot see your illicit pleasure. She climbs naturally, opening up her face to the heavy sun, balancing, twisting, locking her slender calves around the branches as she pulls a quadruped up a fruit tree.

Vispy is above her, of course. Ha ha ha, I reached before you so I can shake the branch for you, sister.

Gravity is unaware of distance or time; she merely follows a single instinct.

When Jeroo falls (the total distance is not more than ten feet, since guava trees do not grow too tall), she is not thrown out of the tree, so her cry leaves tattered consonants along grazed branches, but her dress decides to uphold her decency and uprights her so she lands finally, at the dying end of her scream, on her left foot.

They have to carry her on a handcart because the family

car is away in Bombay, and Vispy hangs on to the branch he was trying to shake, forgotten by the panic rising within the sea in Bordi.

'Buva, Bordi is on the border of Maharashtra and Gujarat.'

'My brother and I are children of borders, one foot here, another there, one of belonging, one of not belonging.'

'I know your language; you don't know mine.'

'We know your civilisation, you don't know ours.'

'We know your calendar, you don't know ours. (We have thirty-one names for thirty-one days!)'

Vispy retreated away from his sister, to a place in a guava tree in his mind where he was alone and not shaking any branch.

His parents could not see the still tree, and every morning the helpless boy saw in their eyes the blame for a sister lying with a shortened leg.

The fall broke Jeroo's left leg, but it created something new and strange inside her skull. Some neural pathways became trench deep; some grew shallow. They heightened her sense of smell and lowered her sense of sight.

Jeroo started wearing spectacles with thick lenses to school, the school in Mumbai, where they banished her, away from Vispy, to avoid further accidents.

She was able to identify the difference in smells of

ordinary objects: she could smell the difference between the colour red and the colour green when she squeezed the pigments out in painting class.

She entered a parallel universe, not accessible to normal human beings.

She would reach home in her aunt's house at Malabar Hill, and know that the maid servant hadn't arrived that day.

She would reach class and know that the teacher had used coloured chalk instead of just white.

On her way to school, she could tell that the bakery had made samosas, not puffs.

Vispy grew up into a sound engineer, but abandoned all contact with his sister, and then his parents, when he shifted to London, blaming her for falling, blaming her for his parents blaming him.

Jeroo travelled to France, to the hallowed Givaudan Perfumery School in Grasse, where she harnessed her guava-tree-fall-induced olfactory genius to pass with distinction.

Her teachers hoped she would create famous perfumes for a famous Parisian luxury house where she interned, and redefine the industry, combining her understanding of the Western and Eastern perfumery styles.

But she returned to India, only because she couldn't bear her parents living alone.

She continued to travel, being in demand at seminars

around the globe, the blurring edge between natural and artificial molecules, the marriage of perfumes and human skin esters to create unique signatures on the human body, the retention rates in cosmetics, the decay rates of smells in shampoos.

Jeroo Jeejebhoy, or JJ, as she was referred to, was the President of the United States of Fragrances.

Eleven

Buva and the Baby

Ten days after he visited Reshma, Buva returns to Sunanda madam at room 308.

She grunts as she rises on her elbow, then straightens her back, rests it against the wall, and closes her eyes, wondering if she did right in setting off a storm.

'Dekha?' Did you see her?

Yes.

She told me something I didn't know. She said she had had my child.

'How do you know it was yours?'

Why would she lie just before…

Just before what? He is unable to complete the thought; it raises a helpless angry red welt in his mind.

Just before she died, don't you understand?

He remembers the smell of the rotting cells and alien drugs in her breath.

'Didn't you ask her?' Sunanda madam has spent so many hours arguing with so many angry, lusty, violent men drawn to her flock, she knows instinctively how to play them.

She knows Buva is not a typical customer; she has witnessed his inner strength from the days of Hanuman Lane and Sadhana Cinema.

She listens to his response.

'She was tired. It was not right to tire her more… I just… Just held her, hoping the black tide of disease would recede.'

Sunanda madam crosses an invisible line between business and compassion, strange bedfellows in Pila House.

These young boys and their dicks. They don't know what drives them. And then they grow up.

This one is six feet tall and built like steel, but his heart, it has stayed soft. Pulpy. So Sunanda madam crosses the line and lays bare the entire catastrophe of Buva's baby.

'Yes, Reshma probably had your child. We all discussed it, all the girls and me, and told her no, mat kar, because whore children have a future like sewage... it flows and moves, but nobody really cares and it is smelly and everybody hates it.'

'But she didn't listen to us, hatti, adiyal, obstinate.'

'She said, "I couldn't change what my parents did to me; they sold me, but I can change the life of a child as a parent."'

'"I can change one life—make my life worth something."'

'We couldn't argue with that. Something to fill this emptiness.'

Then?

'Then?'

'There's no "then" in our profession, Buva. One day at a time. She continued to accept clients. She knew she was pregnant, but she believed she would do good, for the baby. Earning money, saving money.'

'Then one night, one drunk youngster decided to get rough with her... slapped her, kicked her. Must have watched blue movies, no? Tried to strangle her; for her pleasure, he said.'

Buva thinks of that girl in Colaba, bound to a chair.

'We spent three days and nights trying to save her, the baby, bhagwan jaane. Went to the best hospital. Too late, I think. So much blood I have not seen.'

'She got depressed. Like a lifeless doll instead of our

sunshine. Said she will not protect herself. That's how... maybe... the three letters.'

Should he find that young man and demonstrate to him what happens when someone stronger than him chokes him?

Buva stares around the room, disoriented.

Photo of Lord Ganesha, Shah Rukh Khan, brass idols of Lakshmi, Shiva covered with chrysanthemums, stained calendar with large dates, photo of Lord Ganesha.

How do I get off this carousel of pain?

Nothing I do goes untainted. I looked after her. But just when she needed looking after, I was not there.

Twelve

Buva and the Pillion-Rider

Ever since Reshma told him about the child they lost, Buva's anger with women who don't care for their kids on scooters and motorbikes has grown like a fever.

It always existed, but now its edges were turned burning red.

He is on his weekly trip chauffeuring Madam Jeejebhoy, and a sight draws sweat on his forehead.

He freezes.

There, once again, the sight that he can't cope with.

Stop that bloody thing. Be careful on the turn. There is a metallic ting in his forehead, as if the vein is a thin copper pipe being hit by a goldsmith's hammer.

A man riding a scooter, obviously a new rider, concentrating on the traffic ahead, his mouth open in slack concentration. On the pillion, is his wife, wrapped in a slithery nylon sari, sitting sideways, holding a baby in her lap. The baby is playing with the red string of his woollen cap, chubby fingers learning to coordinate the inchoate signals of the synapses in the brain, happy and tranquil, wanting to drag the string into his mouth, happy and absorbed, not aware that the mother holding him is dozing.

When the mother leans forward in her sleep, just a little bit, her lower back muscles straining to hold her spine up, the entire centre of gravity of mother-son goes out of balance, and the scooter wobbles and then keels over. The baby is no longer holding the string. It has not even learnt to put out its arm to prevent injury from the fall. The mother hits the road knee first, then her right arm as her instincts kick in, and then her shoulder. Despite her bulk and silk sari, from somewhere inside her, she realises that if she turns over, she will save her baby from injury, from the merciless stone-hard river of tar.

Buva's cab screeches to a halt five metres away.

He leaps out and runs towards the accident, roaring

incomprehensibly, sweat pouring out of him. Another lady has already reached the mother and helped her heave herself up, so she is sitting on her backside, her legs straight before her. The baby is crying its head off in the arms of another lady who has rushed in to help.

Buva picks the scooter up with one arm, and helps the father up with the other. The father is hobbling but his leg appears straight, no broken bones.

Buva slips the scooter back onto its foot stand, and then holds him up so his face is next to his own, shouting, 'You bloody fool, don't you realise you are carrying a baby?'

Madam Jeejebhoy has extracted herself from the front seat, unable to stay away from the scene of averted tragedy, and walks up to the foursome. She extends an arm to the mother, who uses this support and a hand on her nylon-slithery knee to finally stand up, her shock now turned into relief, kissing and kissing her terrorised little bundle of joy.

Back in the cab, Madam Jeejebhoy asks Buva whether he had foreseen the event, and he tells her how he can spot people who are not aware of their responsibility; he hates people who don't understand responsibility.

'If you are in my Kamandalu, you are my responsibility.'

Why become a father if you want to continue behaving like a son?

The metallic ting in his forehead has subsided, and Buva is worried he has lost too much time. Madam will be late.

'It's okay,' she says, reading his mind, 'once or twice to reach late... helping others is good.'

They continue north through what Buva's nose describes as the Central Corridor of smell.

Mumbai has three seams of smell, like its railway tracks: West Coast, East Coast and Central.

The Central one, where he has to cut in from the West Coast to go to Vikhroli, is away from the sea. This corridor is swamped by the vapours of its predominant produce: Dadar is awash in crushed vegetables in the morning; flowers in the evening. The Chembur air is thick with the refinery and fertilizer-factory effluvia, until they reach the marshes of Vikhroli and the destination at a famous soap factory, with its wall of saponifying oil smell.

'One day I must try driving blindfolded.'

'Remember, Buva,' reminds Madam Jeejebhoy, 'smell is the only human sense that brings floating molecules from our environment into direct contact with our neurons. It is the most naked sense. It has a shortcut; it is not filtered by anything till it reaches the brain, so it stays in the brain forever, samzha?'

Madam Jeejebhoy holds his fingers in hers and lets her

tears flow when he drops her off at the airport: her pain had never found a voice.

She is going to France, to Grasse, where she had studied her fine art and where she has been offered a year's free innovation scholarship.

The only reason for staying on in India was valid no longer: her parents were now confined to an old-age home, unable to recognise her or each other. The best old-age homes are outside the municipal limits of Mumbai, and she has chosen one that is beyond Bhayander, with a manicured garden, exactly as they had had in their echo-empty house in Bordi.

They make an odd sight at midnight, awash in the puky yellow halogen light of the Mumbai airport—a tall, graceful lady with short grey hair, wearing a well-designed suit, leaning slightly on her artificial foot, and a tall muscular man in a white safari suit, with long black hair and a full beard, holding fingers.

She has handed over just one responsibility to him. 'Remember to go and see how they are, once in a while. And call me if you feel there is a problem; doesn't matter what the keepers say.'

Her older brother was still sulking somewhere in London, a reputed sound engineer, blaming his parents and his sister for his guilt.

Madam Jeejebhoy has handed Buva one gift too.

'This I created for you… use it when you want to be reminded of who you are.'

It was a tiny teardrop-shaped Swarowski vial tied at the end of a handcrafted silver necklace.

Once in a while, when the world jostled and crowded out Buva's equanimity, he would take the necklace off, gently pull out the stopper and inhale the complex fragrance of self-respect: a deep base note of a unique oakmoss tautened by hard musk and then made caring and unique with a top note of his favourite sandalwood.

'The first impression of you is this very traditional and Indian sandalwood,' read her invisible telegram to him, 'but as one digs deeper, one discovers a human being so unique, the circumstances that ganged up against you and reduced you to the slumland drop off, and reveal the unshakeable foundation of oakmoss. Celebrate yourself, Buva.'

He remembers the oceanic fragrances she wore, and smiles to himself.

Thirteen

Buva and the Riots

I've watched meaningless caste wars, now I have to live to witness meaningless religious wars.

It's 1992, and the dismantling of the Babri Masjid has triggered riots in Mumbai.

Buva is pissed off by the glass and stones on the road, not good for Kamandalu's tyres.

He has turned to look right at the armoured car on the other side of the road, his sinuses flooded by the dung-like smell of the flowers of the wild almond 'poon' trees that grow mainly along this six-lane artery connecting the dockside nodes, when there is a thud against his cab.

It's a woman. In black.

She is whimpering, her black hijab wrapped around a baby, and she has bumped into Kamandalu because she is looking over her shoulders while running.

Buva rushes out and opens the door on the left for her to get in, while his ears pick up three men running down the lane where she has emerged from, screaming 'Har har Mahadev', their screams fuelling their lust for an easy quarry, the word 'quarry' itself drawing from another language for disembowel.

Yes, yes, yes, a Muslim woman and a child in one single blow of the swords that they are carrying, steel puncturing soft enemy flesh, extracting revenge for wrongs committed many centuries earlier by textbooks and flared-nostrilled raconteurs.

Fucking Muslims overstaying Bharat Maataa's welcome.

Here we come to prove our manhood, since our wimpish national leaders didn't, in 1947.

The metallic ting in Buva's forehead almost blinds him.

Think, Buva, is this your business?

How can a baby being killed not be any human being's business? What is this separation between a Hindu baby and Muslim baby?

'*Me tu ha bhram, upaasanaa hi bhram; ishwarbhaav ha hi bhram, nischayesi.*'

'I and You are illusions, worship is illusion; knowing God is illusion, for certain.'

Buva has opened the boot and extracted his trusted iron rod kept for protection against attacks on Kamandalu even without thinking what he wants to do next.

The woman is sobbing, and in desperation has rolled up the glass on her side of the seat, something, anything to prevent her baby from being cut into pieces. How many hours he had shouldered through the narrow passages between her hip bones to emerge from the warm waters of her womb after two of them had not survived the journey, her husband now desperate, and how eagerly he had suckled her till-then dry nipples and then slept with his fists like soft balls. And now twelve months later, after that pelvic girdle-breaking event, just when he had started calling her Ammi in a gurgling tone, they would hold his head by the hair and slit his throat, but perhaps she will not see that.

To the utter surprise of the three men, who are carrying swords, Buva starts walking towards them, rather than away.

He reaches within striking distance in a couple of strides, stops abruptly, steps to one side, kneels on his right leg and swings the iron rod hard to hit the first man's shins.

The shattered bone can no longer support the momentum of his run and he tumbles past Buva, attempting to break his own fall on the river of tar. The gravel sandpapers his exposed hairy, bulbous stomach. The rusty sword escapes his grip as his fingers crunch between steel grip and road. His breath explodes out of his tobacco- and khaini-smelling mouth.

Out of the other two who have overrun Buva, the second man, who has just barely come to terms with the fact that this man who looks like a Hindu king is actually protecting a Muslim slut, turns with both his arms holding the sword above his head. 'Bhenchod, gaddaar, tuzhya aila...'

The sword is meant to hit Buva's shoulder, separating this gaandu's traitor arm from his sinful body.

Buva explodes up on his surya-namsakar-hardened thigh while switching the rod to a short grip and shoves it upwards into the man's groin, penetrating skin and intestine instantly.

The man's brain is unable to comprehend the gap between the intended hit on the shoulder and the slash through empty space, and as the trauma of steel entering his innards reaches his survival centres, he sinks to the ground.

The third man has almost reached the cab and when he makes the mistake of turning around to check what has happened to his fellow conquerors, he discovers Buva standing upright with his rod in his right arm. The battle is half lost in the man's head because he detects no fear in Buva's eyes; some blood and pinkish flesh has splattered and clung on Buva's white shirt and trousers, and one of his team members is gasping on the road, face down, while the other clutches his torn abdomen.

For a moment, he snarls and holds his sword upright, but the 'Har har Mahadev' becomes a squeak as he sees Buva walking towards him, and then, abandoning all sense of shame, he rushes away, his hardened penis now limp in fear.

Something, anything, please, merciful Allah.

My mother flew through air and landed on rock, and mother-son and mother-daughter are truer than any other classifications in your heads, religion caste class I don't understand, says Buva to himself as he starts Kamandalu and unconsciously heads towards Mohammad Ali Road turning left into Matunga.

'Bhendi Bazaar?' he wants to confirm.

'Yes, I have my brother there, please take me there. I don't want Dilshan to die. My brother will give you whatever you want.' She is half weeping, half laughing amidst the sounds of ambulances and police vans, pulling out three pathetic hundred rupee notes that she hopes will delay further attacks on this farishta, this Hindu angel who has helped Dilshan and her survive the killing.

The mousy politician who triggered these waves of violence with the demolition of a mosque sits in a quiet bungalow writing his memoirs in pink verse.

Fourteen

A Jamboree of Freedom Fighters

The Jamboree Maidan.

This is where charismatic individuals addressed gatherings of poor Indians before India got its freedom, exhorting them to fight against the British.

Strangers jostled for space here, became friends and fellow-fighters, dreaming of an India that gave them respect.

The British in turn created these 122 rock-solid buildings where they could hold the protesters.

They were prisons, not residences.

For some reason, the complex has an abundance of ficus religiosa trees called 'pimpal' in Marathi.

Rain as water threads. Winter as fogged windows on Kamandalu. Summer as birds waking up before him on the thirty-odd ficus religiosa trees amongst the ghetto: whatever the season, Buva walks out to the centre of Jamboree Maidan, along with Kalya, his pet tomcat, who is absent only during the rains.

The maidan was where traditional wrestlers did their pushups against a time-keeper called a candle: they started with a full candle and continued till the candle had extinguished itself, surpassing records, unknown to the Guinness Book.

The Jamboree Maidan has transformed from a platform for driving out foreigners to a platform for building a vote bank.

This is where Buva practises his sun salutation, surya namaskar.

This is where Buva summons all energy, mental, physical, and spiritual.

Stand straight. Become aware of the weight of the body grounded to earth through the soles of the feet; evenly distributed, a straight line piercing fontanelle and tail bone.

The body is a microcosm of the universe.

The palms press against each other on the chest even while the elbows pull back, thrust and anti-thrust in perfect equilibrium.

I am a mountain, a metaphor for stability. Like how the mountain is unfazed by headstrong winds and insidious streams stripping its skin, I am unfazed by titillation of circumstance.

Arms above the head, wrists facing each other and touching, biceps brushing ears, the cylindrical cage of ribs thrusting against the planar skin, the gluteus maximus tightened, holding the massive pelvic bone in place to lower the centre of gravity. Bend but retain straightness of spine, bend at the pelvic joint.

I am a half-moon, a metaphor for tension held in abeyance.

Hold breath, let transparent air balloon within transparent lung bags, while the oxygen is busily traded for carbon monoxide.

Bend forward from waist as the rectus femoris muscles hook the kneecaps and tuck them up, the three muscles of the hamstring stretched across the tenterhooks, breath released slowly, an offering to the river of time, palms now resting on the ground next to the feet, soft beard hair against knee.

I am gravity's bow, a metaphor for potential power.
Inhale.

The morning smells jostle through the narrow gangways of the nostrils: the permanent gutter-rot steam, thin powdery tendrils of sandalwood vapouring out of his own body, unruly South Indian coffee whiffs from the home of the Nairs.

I am a monkey, spine and right leg stretched prehensile.

Right foot extends behind, pelvis pushed down, inside of arms coiled tight, head pulling spine up in an arc, arms twist naturally so elbows face the front.

I am a dog, a metaphor for undying loyalty.

Left foot extends behind, a jackknife held in place by wire rope of sinew. Hold breath, the air trapped in the sacs still even as the buttocks rise to imitate a canine play bow.

Spine straight yet, a polymer chain of rough stone converted into a ramrod, taut in space, feet flat on the ground, stretching the biceps femoris and semitendinosus making the gigantic sciatic nerve stretch taut.

I am the eight-point animal.

Down now, shoulder blades kissing each other, pectorals stretched like tapering fleshwings, wrists deliciously extended showing off a delta of veins.

I am a snake, a metaphor for rebirth and purification.

Kalya decides this is the moment to walk across Buva's back—a rough surface of soft pads, leaves, and cloverleaf rangoli on dark brown skin.

Up again and repeat the cycle backwards. Five breaths, twelve poses, each cycle of twelve poses lasts twelve minutes.

The body is a microcosm of the universe.

If you can't experience it in here, you can't experience it outside anywhere, ever.

Fifteen

Buva and the Collector

hile the English-speaking India wraps its early morning arguments in phrases like 'compassionate microfinance' and 'sustainable credit' and its inevitably arrogant venture capitalists populate cocktail circuits pitching the Omidyar for-profit model versus the Bill Gates not-for-profit model, Karim Khan makes sure Buva accompanies him on his carefully planned 'journey cycle' every month.

Unknown to most bankers, finance experts and MBAs churning out strategically insightful PowerPoint presentations,

Karim Khan's model is sustainable, because his model is chained to primordial fear.

Karim needs no collateral; he dispenses cash that is safe because it is untraceable, but noncompliance in returning the interest or the capital usually ends in the borrower losing some part of his anatomy as an initial warning and then, probably, his life, in an unavoidable accident on the teeming railway lines, hit by a train because he tripped while crossing, his body twisted around his thirty-six-boned spine by the impact beyond recognition, or falling on the merciless gravel face down destroying his identity while bending to adjust his sandal as he stands at the outermost ring of the bulging beehive of human beings in Dadar Fast at 6.31 p.m.

There are other avenues of death, crafted to leave no trace of reason why. Buva once watched Karim Khan squeeze the testicles of a man until he gasped his last breath.

The Mumbai Police has never been able to trace the weak clues from bodies of middle-aged men strangled to death and left to rot in uninhabited places in Aarey Milk Colony, Sasunavghar, Sion Fort, or in the most obvious places like the men's room at VT station.

There is no pattern to the identities of the victims.

Karim needs a trustworthy lieutenant, and Buva has been playing that role for over five years now.

They have an unwritten pact: agree on responsibilities, and then don't ask questions.

Buva will not be an accomplice in the life-death chess game; his sole role is to guard the cash when Karim goes on his collections.

Karim comes and drops sacks of notes on the cab floor or in the boot, and Buva stands outside, the iron rod now on the front seat.

But unbelievably, there hasn't been a single incidence of anyone attempting to steal from the collector.

Their day usually ends in Bhayendar, out of Mumbai city's four toll gates, beyond the Ghodbunder Check Post, with Nafeesa, Karim's favourite transvestite.

The Kismet Resort has been created just outside city limits for truck drivers, moneyed suburban businessmen whose fantasies cannot be fulfilled by their straitlaced wives (or at least that's what the poor husbands presumed) and skittish teenagers on their first coupling driven by the smell of smegma and DNAs attempting to replicate.

In the beginning, Karim would spend time with Nafeesa inside Kamandalu, but soon realised that his trusted accomplice was uncomfortable with the arrangement.

When the rendezvous started getting longer, Buva found other pursuits: opposite the resort was an ancient temple and beyond that, as one climbed up, unclaimed or abandoned vegetable patches, and two old water tanks.

Buva ended up sitting next to one of these tanks, muscular thighs resting against unyielding stone, legs dangling over the edge, and then sometimes, when the water and the tank triggered a faint scream uncoiling inside his head, he would get up.

Sixteen

Sylvia and the Benefactor

S tanley always asked Sylvia to come after 11 a.m. to his home in Pasta Lane because that's when his day began, after his late-night parties, after he had chilled his alcohol-soaked body in his AC bedroom.

He preferred to pay her cash, instead of a cheque, her monthly dole, to look after her son and daughter, after his best friend Vernon died in an inexplicable accident.

'How, Sylvia, how? I can't believe it even now!'

'No other guest has ever fallen over... I am famous for being careful.'

'He did a lot for me, Vernon, he did a lot... this is my duty.'

He would repeat that sentence every time they met.

In the first few months, he would let her in, politely request her to sit, go into the inner room and return with the cash.

Respect and distance and a formal smile.

On one of her visits, the rather neatly dressed darwan called her.

'Memsaab!'

When she turned, he came up to her and told her Stanley was not home today.

'But come up... something there is... for you.'

He accompanied her up to the flat, stood aside politely to let her in. She could smell the heavy attar on his body.

She found the money lying in an envelope.

As months passed, Stanley started requesting her to sit down and have some tea.

Thank you, Stanley, for all the help.

You are filling up many hollows. In stomachs, in hearts, in wallets.

'Yes, the kids are doing fine. I am able to save enough for their school fees. I don't know what I would do without this.' She limply waves the envelope. 'I have no skill... is there any job I could do?'

Stanley tells her to wait till the children have grown up. They must be missing their dad, they must settle down with her. They must be missing him, no?

'Yes, he used to spoil them silly.'

'We will find a job for you then, when they won't miss you much, hmmm?'

On her next few visits, she insisted on making the tea herself in his huge kitchen, her gesture of conciliation and respect: it held a large freezer, big enough to hold his entire cache of illegal material.

Later, he started bringing her gifts. Don't mind, Sylvia, you can't just live on bread alone. Dear Lord, give us this day our daily bread. Or something else, if Vernon was around.

'I was in Dubai last week with a client. There was this gold festival; I thought who would it look nice on?'

The gold wrist band is shaped like a snake, and it coils around her wrist, but she does not heed its warning.

'Here, Vernon told me you like burgundy lipstick.'

'Also, please don't call me sir. Vernon was just five years, I think, younger to me.'

Then there is this day in the middle of July, the rain is a liquid wall through which you can barely see a few feet away, and when she enters, chilled to the bone, she can sense the difference in the room.

He had already bathed and was wearing a fresh T-shirt, pulled hard over his muscular chest, pulled hard around the slight bulge of his rock-hard belly.

While she was preparing the tea, he stood behind her, and placed his hand on her shoulder.

'Sylvia, you don't feel lonely... two years, no? You can't live on bread alone.'

She gasped.

No, says her mind.

Yes, says the hoopoe in the Vasai Fort, yes and yes, up and down his head went. Many parts of her young body are starved, their memories smouldering under the ashes of Vernon's memories.

No, says her mind, Vernon never did anything like this.

His second hand is now resting on her other shoulder, the warmth seeping into her body, loosening knots, sending wake-up alarms, moistening surfaces.

I am sorry, Vernon, it was you who trained my body for this celebration of the senses.

Thank you, Stanley, for filling many hollows, some that Vernon alone filled.

In the chill of his bedroom, her body wakes up again.

Stanley brushes her nostrils with a white powder, without waiting to ask her permission.

The cocaine infiltrates her. It is like a drug customised

for her long history in Vasai: her fragile ego experiences euphoria, then the confidence to be herself, and then the ease of being sociable.

In bed, Stanley is far less gentle, but over the months, she develops an appetite for his roughness. There are many doors inside her, each leading further down, and she gives in to the relentless temptation of opening them.

Blindfolded, a million signals from her two-and-a-half-inch deep explode inside the darkness in her head.

Her monthly visits become weekly. She is getting addicted to the cocaine. There are no warning signals. The world is right, after such a long time. After years.

Then, one day, just as she was careening over the edge with the crimson tide inside her head, he whispers, 'Am I as good as Vernon?'

Her giggle is trapped in her throat.

Over time, she understands the deeper meaning of that question. Stanley has been patient in the way he has laid the trap.

First respect, then lust, now contempt: she opened one door after another for him, allowing him to follow her into a dark chamber smelling of must.

She knots the anger into a ball, a girl without parents who experienced sunshine from a husband who could use his body like nobody else could, only to realise that the sunshine was actually floodlights to record her defenceless self on a brutally shared camera.

The months pass, and Stanley keeps mistaking Sylvia's beleaguered silence for acquiescence.

Stanley then whispers the most painful secret of all, while she is hog-tied.

'Why do you need a job…you are doing fine…after all, Vernon did the same.'

'Vernon did the same.'

No, that's another lie. He did not drink; he did not womanise. He created a dance for me and called it Sylventine.

No, this is another lie.

'Didn't he tell you why he was so much in demand on my ship parties? Not just for his dancing, come on, grow up, silly slut Sylvia!'

'Didn't you realise where the gifts came from? All those expensive gifts your children and you enjoyed so many times?'

Did he steal the lipstick from a rich socialite he was having sex with?

'Are you saying you really haven't heard of the term? Gigolo?'

'He was a male whore, Sylvia.'

She shakes her head, returns to her home in Mahim, maimed physically and emotionally.

Used, cheated, humiliated: she shouldn't have fallen prey to her own flesh.

Vernon had cheated twice over.

And now Stanley was doing the same.

She had to find a way of breaking out of this prison of silk.

No skills, no job, no future, two children.

It's either escape and revenge, or just escape, or just revenge.

What will you choose, Shrinking Violet?

The hoopoe waits for your answer.

Seventeen

Buva and Shivthar Ghal

The riots have stirred too much muck at the bottom of his mind.

Buva needs his yearly retreat to Shivthar Ghal, the womb in the mountain where his hero Swami Samarth Ramdas composed the magnificent song over twelve long years.

When the unkempt ST bus drops him off at Barasgaon, just a few kilometres after Mahad on the Mumbai–Goa highway, fifteen kilometres off Shivthar Ghal, Buva feels the transformation.

He changes into an orange dhoti and khadaus, wooden clogs stuck to his feet because of the single knob jutting between his big toe and middle.

He is bare-bodied, skin kissed by the green moisture in the air.

He will walk the next fifteen kilometres, slowly losing weight off his mind: Mumbai sloughs off, childhood sloughs off, pain sloughs off.

His skin changes colour, absorbing the dark red of the soil.

The hillocks are soft green upheavals of an earth eager to drink in the impending monsoon. Buva's nose rejoices in the exotic cocktail of smells: cow dung, marigold, smoke.

He walks steadily, covering five kilometres every hour. He has carried no water or food.

When he finally reaches the gentle slope leading to the waterfall, his mind has grown into a pinpoint.

The noise of the waterfall is a curtain too, and behind that curtain is a cave system.

This is where Swami Samarth Ramdas sat for twelve years and wrote his masterpiece along with his faithful follower, Kalyan Swami.

This is where I will sit for twelve days and read it and let the words dissolve the barriers within me.

The secretary of Shivthar Ghal Sundarmath Seva Samiti

leads him to his room, since he has been a regular visitor who needs no introduction.

Buva leaves his bag in the room, and returns to the cave with the bigger edition of *Dasbodh*.

A youngster bows to him instinctively; in the half light, a tall man wearing an orange dhoti, having coal-black hair and beard is a startling sight.

He sits close to the likenesses of Swami Samarth Ramdas and his student, Kalyan Swami, and starts humming the shlokas to himself. He discovers another voice intersecting his, and realises there is an old lady sitting ten feet away, with the same copy as his.

'Prapaate...' 'In the waterfall...'

The wet light filtering through the waterfall dances on her silver hair. Human beings acquire unforeseen powers in pursuit of the unknown. There are myths about the eight primary siddhis.

An hour later, she touches his head affectionately as she walks past him to the dining area. 'Buva, there is a black river running inside your soul. Allow it to overflow, or let it dry up.'

He sits there, glued ashamed to the uneven rock.

What did she know and how?

How would you know, Buva? Better to stick to what your guru told you.

For the next twelve days, Buva follows a strict regimen: he increases the number of surya namaskars to 108, has frugal meals, a twenty-minute nap in the afternoon, seven hours of sleep at night and sits in meditation the rest of the time, unmoving, the sound of the waterfall entering his consciousness and washing away all thought.

Death, deceit, disease.

All washed away.

Maybe someday, I should settle down here.

Eighteen

Sylvia and the Darwan

For the third time in six months, Stanley is not at home.

The darwan repeats his polite routine, never giving her the key, accompanying her to the flat on the third floor, climbing behind her, leaving the door open for her to step in and discover the money on the living room table.

This time he steps in and locks the door behind him.

'Memsaab!'

'What is this? What are you doing?... You mad?... Go out!'

'Memsaab, your husband Vernon?'

Yes. How did he know?

'Yes, was. Died. Dead. What do you want? Get out... I will tell Stanley.'

She shrinks, and steps back. But he does not move.

'He fight with Stanley before died.'

'What?'

'Memsaab, building fisherman told me. At night, big fight here. Vernon and Stanley. big fight. Then go to big yacht. Then die.'

'Means what, what are you saying?'

'Memsaab, don't know, fisherman say Stanley kill husband.'

She lies in her bed in her house in Mahim, chest constricted, whorls of darkness choking her. Her son and daughter no longer sleep next to her; they sleep by themselves in the living room.

I was happy being Shrinking Violet, being a nobody in a once-glorious Portuguese town now lying in ruins.

Then six years of sunshine, thinking that a husband who was a star loved me and my children.

Then in three years, the men in my life have stripped me, layer after layer: first self-respect, then trust, then shame.

I am a toy. I have no money, no future, no escape.

I lie in the ruins of the fort, blamed by the hoopoe—
why did you say yes, like I do?

I have read in newspapers why people commit suicide.
Maybe I should.

Maybe I should try to find another idea.

Nineteen

Buva and Inspector Pethe

The Ear Nation's wisdom believes our body goes through two twelve-hour circadian rhythms, not one twenty-four-hour one.

At four in the morning is when the body has its lowest energy physically, and at its highest energy spiritually.

The Eye Nation believes the same, but its thesis does not include the spiritual dimension.

So most arrests take place at four in the morning, when the suspected criminal is drifting on the ebbing tide of consciousness, body slack, nerves relaxed, snoring open-mouthed.

It is Kalya who responds to the entry of the policemen carrying their antiquated .303 rifles.

Buva is disturbed by his hiss and opens his eyes two hours before his stipulated time, staring up the long barrel of a rifle in the half luminescence seeping in through the window from a misbehaving tubelight

'Under arrest... murder,' says the policeman, while outside, Inspector Prakash Pethe stands with his arms crossed, unable to end the battle between the left arm of his duty and the right hand of this act of treason, his jaws trying to clamp down the rising anger against himself.

Ten seconds pass while Buva assimilates the news.

Then he folds his hands in a namaste and says, 'Give me two minutes to myself.'

The policeman backs off, but stands blocking the door.

Buva picks Kalya up, cuddles him and kisses his head. 'Don't worry, everything will be OK. You stay here; somebody will feed you.'

He bends down in obeisance before Swami Samarth Ramdas's photo, then removes from around his neck the vial of perfume Madam Jeejebhoy had gifted to him and places it near the photo frame.

Two policemen wait for him to come out, ready to escort him by holding his palms interlocked with theirs because the Crime Manual as well as the Supreme Court mandate says that you can't use handcuffs without a magistrate's permission. A third policeman opens up the lone trunk in the room: it contains everything that Buva ever possessed.

One photograph of his maternal uncle who brought him to Mumbai, his wooden khadaus, slippers he uses when walking to and residing in Shivthar Ghal, his cloth bag for Shivthar Ghal, and his big version of *Dasbodh*.

It certainly does not have anything that the policeman was looking for. What was he looking for?

Buva leaves the door unlocked. Maybe young Shalini or someone like her will need it.

Sushitai the nurse has gotten up early for her shift at the hospital. She is carrying water from the communal tap, and the sight of Buva being held by two policemen on either side makes her drop her large copper pot in sheer terror.

The sound echoes down the long stone corridor, riding her involuntary questioning and angry scream, mustered out of all her affection for this gentle giant, 'Buva?'

By the time the police reach the opening of the corridor, they face a wall of human beings, shocked into high alert by the oddity of seeing Buva, strangely with his palms entwined with the palms of two pot-bellied policemen on either side of him, head unbowed yet accepting these antics of fate wordlessly.

The crowd knows Inspector Prakash Pethe: he is one of their own. The boy who studied in school and college instead of fighting gang wars, the boy who Buva had nurtured and protected all his life.

Inspector Pethe is leading the three policemen and Buva out of Worli BDD chawl number 43.

Pakya stands in the centre of the seemingly immovable human wall, scratching his limp right arm, his tone casual yet menacing.

He makes sure he does not demean his friend Prakash by calling him by his first name.

'Saheb, what?'

'Don't make trouble, Pakya, murder suspect... serious... it's not aaltu-faltu gang war.'

The policeman holding Buva's entwined palm gets a stinging slap on the back of his head.

So does the second policeman.

And the third.

Then one more, and one more.

It's called 'tapli' and in normal BDD chawl life is meant to be a casual tap of affection, but this one is not.

The policemen know they shouldn't react. BDD Chawls are known for their lack of fear of the law; they stare ahead, jaws clenched. Maybe their Inspector Pethe knows how to deal with this ugly mob.

Inspector Pethe knows he has to control the situation through words, rather than force.

His voice is loud but his tone is sincere.

'Listen, I know Buva is innocent, but a man has filed an FIR about his brother's murder in Colaba. What do you prefer? That I take him to custody rather than any other inspector... at least I know how to respect Buva... like you all do... OK, barobar?'

There is silence as the mob absorbs his logic.

Then he says something to the crowd that ends the stalemate.

'Pakya will meet me later after my duty hours...'

There is a tacit implication that BDD chawls will know the truth, beyond the law, through their own inspector son, in the voice of their brainiest khabri, Pakya.

Reluctantly, the crowd dissolves, but several follow Buva to the van.

For the first time, when the procession reaches the van, Buva speaks.

Everything he says is about taking care of others.

'Sushitai, please feed Kalya. There is money in the cupboard for fish.'

'Pakya, inform Jeroo memsaab in France, and Joshi Mai at Worli Sea Face, Shalini's broker... I can't come any longer.'

Then he whispers to Pakya, 'Karim also.'

Pakya waits till the van dissolves into a dripping steel mass in his tearful eyes, and then returns to his room, pulls out his trusted machete, walks out into the dawn and starts hacking his favourite carrom board, twenty-nine inches of lacquered plywood, the tiny coliseum of his identity, roaring expletives in anger, with tears streaming down his face.

'Maadarchod! I will tear you apart, limb by limb, when I find you, I will tear you apart, limb by limb.'

He saved me from being killed by those Currey Road bastards; he saved that Muslim baby from three sword-wielding motherfuckers, single-handedly—how can he kill anybody? Who are you, framing him? I will tear you apart.

It takes two men including Unni the giant to hold him back from killing the imaginary person who he believes has framed Buva.

Shalini, the lemon-juice selling youngster, has slept through nurse Sushitai's scream and is woken up much later by the unusual silence wrapping the stone chawl.

Her face turns white when she understands that she is an orphan once more.

Kalya sits on the window sill, still, aware that there is something unusual happening to the man who has been his friend for twelve years.

Kalya is getting old now; cats rarely live beyond sixteen.

Twelve. The number of years Swami Samarth Ramdas walked around India, understanding how oppressors oppressed, meeting the Sikh Warrior Guru Hargobind, understanding the essence of being a hermit inside and a warrior outside.

Twelve. The number of years Swami Samarth Ramdas took to write his epic treatise *Dasbodh*.

Twelve. The number of surya namaskars Buva does every day, two sets of twelve (legend has it that his guru used to do nine sets, a total of 108).

Twelve. The number of names of the Sun God one must remember while performing the surya namaskars.

How long will Buva be in jail?

The average number of years undertrials spend in jail in India is… twelve.

That evening, in the carrom room of Bhogadevi Sports Club, locked from inside, Prakash Pethe and Pakya sit with two 750 ml bottles of McDowell's No. 1 whisky.

One mind trained to doubt every shred of evidence, the other trained to soak in everything that does not look like evidence.

His name?

Stanley D'Souza.

Owns a booze shop in Colaba. Involved in brawls before. The Colaba Police Station avoids getting on the wrong side of Stanley: lot of influence among the fishermen community who get booze subsidised for the Army and Navy every night through him. Old Monk costs 450 rupees outside, 200 rupees from him. Has a boat permanently moored at Sassoon Dock: you can get whatever you want at any time of day and night. Even fashionable South Bombay types access him in the early morning for their after-parties: booze, hash, cocaine.

Stanley was known to have done similar business in Goa and across the harbour, in Alibag, so his fellow workers are used to his absence.

But Stanley's brother Sinclair D'Souza, from London, had not heard from him for a month, which was unusual. So he called his friends at the Colaba Police Station. That's when they landed up at Stanley's house.

And?

And broke down the door and found him stuffed inside a big ice-cream freezer that he had in his kitchen... the flats in Colaba are huge. That's why there was no smell of putrefaction, no clue to the killing.

Motive?

Sinclair D'Souza, from London, told the police he heard of a cab driver from Sylvia, a lady Stanley helped every month. She told the police that when she was paying Buva the money for the cab, he saw bundles of cash lying on the bed. So he rang the bell again and broke into the house by breaking the chain.

But why did he kill the owner of the flat?

She informed the police that the man pulled his gun to fight back for the cash, but Buva must have overpowered him and killed him.

She saw Buva killing the man? Strangled him? Broke his skull?

No, Buva had tied her and blindfolded her.

What did the postmortem reveal?

His body may have been stuffed in the freezer when he was unconscious: there is a wound on the back of his head.

Why was Sylvia in that building in Colaba if she stays in Worli?

Stanley was a well-wisher who supported her children's education; her husband was Stanley's friend, but he died two years ago. She had gone to collect her children's fees.

Proof?

The fingerprints on the pistol kept on the sofa that had the cash.

But how did they connect to Buva?

The darwan Santosh Singh remembered him... very difficult to miss Buva.

He testified to the police too.

He also mentioned the woman. Sylvia Pereira. That she used to come every week to meet Stanley.

Then that 'Kamandalu' written in rainbow colours on his cab. And the Kailash Parbat guy said he looked disturbed and did not finish his meal.

And finally, today, the fingerprints on the pistol matched Buva's.

So the police has to file a charge sheet and take him to court tomorrow.

Inspector Pethe gulps down a huge peg.

'When they described Kamandalu, I had a hole in my stomach. But I had to tell the Colaba Police Station the truth.'

They have finished the first bottle, and it's Inspector Pethe's turn to lose self-control and go maudlin.

'Bhenchod, he bought me my entire set of SSC books and gave them to me on the first day of night school, and the books for college, and then I go and get him put behind bars!'

He smashes his glass against the wall.

'All these fucking women... cunt traps!'

Pakya remembers the road known as SSC Road on the western side of the BDD chawls, parallel to Madame Cama Road, where every year, eager students would sit in the light under the lampposts concentrating on their studies, not for the light, but to stay away from the drunken wife-beating brawls at home.

Despite the booze sloshing in every brain cell, Pakya has several questions:

Where is the cash, then, if not found with Buva?

(Did Buva give it to Karim Khan? Inspector Prakash Pethe does not know who Karim Khan is, so the question is never articulated by Pakya.)

The darwan who remembered Buva and the woman—what else did he know?

If she came every week, she obviously did not come for her children's fees.

The inspector composes himself, opens the second bottle, and reveals the final secret:

Her testimony says Buva threatened to kill her son and daughter if she told anybody about what had happened. He made sure she reached home in his own cab, so that she wouldn't go to the police.

Twenty

Buva and Darkness

C an light emerge out of darkness?
*'Dehabhimaan, karmaabhimaan... mokshaabhimaan...
ya naav bhram.'*

'Pride about your body, pride about your achievements,
even pride about being liberated.... Even the pride associated
with the idea of liberation is illusion.'

The first day stretches every nerve in Buva's body.

He has been put along with Class C prisoners, 120
undertrials stuffed in a cell that could fit forty.

Forget kurmaasan, Buva has no space to sit in his
meditation pose.

At night, there is no space to sleep on your back. Everybody sleeps sideways, just to be able to touch the floor.

The room singes Buva's olfactory nerve.

Unwashed, sweaty men, unwashed feet, feet covered in human dung, since the toilet is merely a hole surrounded by human crap, the only way to relieve yourself is to crouch with your feet in the crap.

By an amazing feat, all walls are covered with red paan spit, right up to the ceiling. How did they manage this?

Buva stays away from the so-called toilet, wondering how he will manage in the days to come: he had put away his secret vial of calmness given by Madam Jeejebhoy when he got arrested.

Thankfully, Inspector Prakash Pethe is experiencing a minor redemption after his sinful arrest of Buva. He has been able to bribe the prison in charge and get Buva transferred to the Class B section of the prison on the next day—which means only four prisoners in one barred cage, a hard but clean stone bed to sleep on and a relatively clean toilet.

Best luxury of all: a bath every two days.

Buva is able to do his surya namaskars at the crack of dawn, and his meditation at night.

The other prisoners are unable to pigeonhole Buva.

Is he putting on an act, or has he really retracted himself from the external world?

He is polite to all, friendly with none.

Then stories of his acts start filtering in.

What he did during the riots, what he did during the caste wars in BDD chawls, what he did with the police.

You may be in a prison, but its walls cannot cage stories about you.

At a time when at least two Dalit houses were set on fire every day, Buva's mother's killing wasn't even disturbing the statistics; she had committed suicide due to domestic violence.

Your angry father set your mother on fire, boy, that's the truth according to government records—and then himself, in repentance.

Buva stays alone, trying to physically bend the long hours to his mental and spiritual discipline. How many days, months, years? His icon spent twelve years just writing down the most enduring book of all times for him.

This is nothing. I am innocent. I will find a way out.

The first month is uneventful.

Buva is classified as a neutral non-interfering 'party' by the hardened undertrials.

He appears interesting in what he does, with those twenty-four surya namaskars wherever he finds space, and his hour-long meditation in the dirtiest corner, unmoving, even his eyelids don't flutter.

He is no threat; he provides no great political connections to the outside world, a conduit to privileges denied to the throng of undertrials: from air-conditioned rooms to homemade food to individual toilets.

There are even a couple of youngsters who ask to be taught this great yogic practice, the sun salutation.

It is a morning like any other, where they stand in a queue for the thin milky tea and two slices of bread. A burly man with a beard dyed mehendi-red wearing an Afghani kurta reaches out and snatches the bread and tea glass from a youngster before him.

The youngster is in shorts and nothing else: there is a rumour that you can sell your clothes for booze or hash.

When the youngster curses him, the man frees up his hands by placing the two glasses on the counter and slaps the youngster hard, his face expressionless. The boy is sent sprawling on the sticky floor of the canteen.

Buva winces inwardly. This is none of your business; you focus on getting out of this web of deceit you are trapped in.

How can anything not be anybody's business?

It was the final stages of the gang war between the Worli BDD chawls and the Currey Road BDD chawls.

In a grey dusk that would soon be smeared blood-red and crimson, Arun Kumbhar's buxom, newly married sister

Swapna was walking down the Currey Road bridge, and the boy she had spurned to settle instead for an 'arranged marriage', Suresh Dhasal, from the Currey Road BDD chawls, had, while going past her on his scooter, squeezed her backside and said something so obscene, she couldn't even narrate it to her brother, Arun.

Arun Kumbhar, a five-foot-nothing ball of rage, face carrying a vertical purple scar from a previous encounter, was planning to go alone, armed with his trusted sword, when Pakya stopped him and explained simply, 'You are not going there to die for Swapna, you are going there to kill for her... so let me plan the attack.'

They put together a mean team, just four of them, armed with old tubelights, bulbs filled with hydrochloric acid, swords and Pakya's favourite 'chopper', a solid machete guaranteed to cut through a human femur.

The Currey Road boys had just downed their first shots of naringi, the state-sponsored alcohol in Madhura Desi Bar, the local pub sheltered from the busy street by soiled curtains drawn taut on thin steel springs. The tables were uneven, and outside, Langda Lalit had set up his neatly stacked globular minarets of boiled eggs and pyramids of boiled gram mixed with chopped onions and coriander and chillies, delicately balanced on a wicker stand, illuminated by a thick-wicked kerosene lamp.

Today, business will be good; the youngsters are in a whoopee mood.

Suresh Dhasal's story of 'pom-pomming' was just getting circulated, and the air was getting festive.

'What the fuck... swear on god! Are you saying? Sweet revenge... that hoity-toity bitch... saali!'

'But she needs worse. She needs to be tied up in front of her faggot husband, and...' the rest of the sentence is enacted with great vigour.

Entire tables collapse in vicarious pleasure; the primal male brain is alive and thriving, untouched by so-called civilisation.

The Worli BDD boys, under Pakya, had planned a simple strategy: fast in, fast out.

Hit only Dhasal and retreat, forget injuring or hurting more of his gang or launching a wide-fronted assault.

Pakya knew where their watering hole was, and had expected them to be celebrating Suresh's cheap antics. If we don't find him there, we return and strike another day.

They were emboldened further by the simple fact of having Kamandalu as their vehicle. The pact with Buva was simple. He would never get involved in the gang war. But he was the best bet in any war, to drive in and out.

Today, Buva was on their side.

What more would any gang want?

So when Pakya rushed into the dim interiors of Madhura Bar, his luck favoured him twice over.

He spotted Suresh Dhasal right away: he rushed at him and chopped at his right arm with his heavy chopper as it lay on the table holding his second drink.

Take that, you motherfucker, for pom-pomming our sister.

The blood spurted into the glass. His arm lay connected to the rest of his body with a few white tendrils. Suresh's scream mixed with and congealed the laughter of his friends midair. The bartender reached for his phone to call the police. By the time the others could push back their chairs, struggle to their feet, grasp the audacity of the attack, Pakya had twirled back and extricated himself from the unsteady chairs and tables, and joined his three friends waiting at the door.

Fast in, fast out.

Except Pakya's luck ran out on the street. He ran bang smack into another bunch of Currey Road boys, who, having heard of some celebration at Madhura, were skipping and prancing towards it.

There were roughly seven seconds left before the police arrived or before Pakya could be killed without external wounds, just through the brutal stomping of the Currey Road gang.

How can anything not be anybody's business?

For the umpteenth time in his life, Buva abandoned his reserve and decided to help someone weaker than him.

The five Currey Road boys were kicking Pakya, who bleated in pain, and Arun and the two other boys from Worli were attempting to break the scuffle, and the siren was already keening, and passengers who had just alighted from the train at Currey Road suburban railway station had already frozen in their tracks, when the entire balance of the encounter was tilted by a seventy-five-kilogram giant. Buva bent down, piledrove and shouldered aside three of the boys, plucked Pakya up like a straw doll, grabbed his chopper, ran back to Kamandalu, flung him on the front seat and kept shouting for Arun and the others, who hung on to the open doors of the cab swinging on their hinges, landed safely inside and were off under the Fiat's second gear.

It had cost Pakya one broken rib and six months in custody, but as usual, the code of honour between the gangs meant no witnesses would testify in court, so everyone is out for lack of evidence.

Pakya had done to Suresh Dhasal what the poliomyelitis virus had done to him.

The third morning, in the jail, the young boy attempts to hit back the Afghani kurta-clad guy. What follows is brutal. The man picks the boy up and flings him against the wall, still without speaking a word or without any sign of emotion.

For the first time in three months, the inmates hear Buva's voice.

'Why?'

Nobody answers.

Was the kurta-clad giant a frustrated pedophile?

Did the boy refuse sexual advances?

Did the giant just love throwing his weight around as a sport, bored out of his mind?

He was Ahmed Khan, gang lord from Kurla, gratuitous violence was his favourite weapon for spreading terror. He too was an undertrial without parole, and had made this jail his own empire.

Thus it comes to pass that the next day, Buva stands in between the young boy and the henna-bearded man in the queue.

The whole canteen is watching without watching.

Is it time for another jail murder? Ahmed Khan himself need not touch Buva. Indian jails are full of slashers on hire, who will attack victims for a fee. For cigarettes, for booze, for food.

From somewhere behind the henna-man, another short man jumps the queue, comes between the youngster in shorts and Buva while the henna-man tries to move ahead of both of them.

This move doesn't work.

Buva physically picks up the intruder before him and places him aside and returns to his position in the queue.

After a long time, Buva's senses are on red alert, his massive shoulders tightened, waiting for a blow.

But Ahmed Khan does not say or do anything to Buva.

The inmates wait for the night and the next day, but nothing happens.

On the third day after Buva's confrontation, Ahmed Khan walks up to him.

The arm of the man serving breakfast stops midair.

Ahmed Khan reaches out and places his hand on Buva's shoulder.

'Buvabhai, I did not know about your courage during the riots. Maaf karo, pardon me.'

They hug: a rare gesture for Ahmed Khan.

Pakya's machinations have worked.

He had kept a tab on Buva and had heard of a likely encounter and ensured the news about the woman Buva saved during the riots reached Ahmed Khan.

Ahmed Khan has a gift for Buva: his favourite Cow brand of lime and tobacco.

After several months, the green vine snake of adrenalin slithers up Buva's brain, quietening him even more than ever.

Twenty-one

JJ and Vanilla

Here I am, angry at a system that stares back with deadened eyes.

Thankfully, the system responds to money.

Rupees ten thousand for a better prison cell, or for homemade food to reach you, or for clean linen.

For one full year, Buva hovered around my parents; nobody else could be trusted for being there, and here I am, powerless to help him.

His ebony head stays bowed.

'Look up, Buva, you have done nothing. I believe you.'

How to get him out? She unconsciously touches her spectacles, as she is wont, when she is nervous.

Buva's head continues to be bowed. Trapped. Trapped by his caste not of his making, trapped by a prostitute not of his making, trapped despite wanting to be free as Swami Ramdas.

'Buva, think. Remember. What smell? In the lane? In the cab? Coming? Going?'

'Chanel, Chanel No. 5.'

'Then on the way back?'

'Ice cream.'

'Think harder, Buva; there is no smell called ice cream.'

'Vanilla, yes, vanilla.'

'Yes, vanilla is a smell, Buva....'

Thus is solved one of the most interesting murder mysteries in Mumbai High Court.

A mystery about murder and an easy woman through the smell of a pod that gets its name from the Latin for vagina.

Appropriate, no?

Appropriate also that it is Jeroo Jeejebhoy, President of the United States of Fragrances, who prises open the case based on a smell.

Jeroo Jeejebhoy also discovers that Buva can come out on bail if he has no previous history of crime reported against him.

Time to act.

Twenty-two

Lawyer Sonawane and Light

As Sonawane crouches in what is fashionably now known in the West as well as in the posh new gyms in Eye Mumbai as an Indian Squat on the public latrine hole in his Currey Road BDD chawl, his knees cracking under the tension, the voice of his senior rises higher than the hurried explosion emanating from his anus.

He is no longer worried about what his neighbours in the queue will hear when last night's chana and paneer starters emerge from his body.

'Ek hi chance milega, Sonawane, ek hi!'

'Life will grant you just one big chance, Sonawane, just one,' says his senior in court.

If you can do something with that chance, and remember that chance will not even be clear when it spreads its legs for you, but if you can, then you will escape this trajectory of a small-time prosecutor and become a star.

Once your photo and quote appear in a newspaper, life will change.

Sonawane knows who he is up against: Ujwal Shinde, star government prosecutor, the man who snared the most powerful terrorists and the most powerful celebrity criminals.

Sonawane smiles as his intestine pushes out the last vestige of the night before.

That tall lady, with a false leg, and that Pakya, with one arm, the police khabri, and him, had spent the night before in that quarter-system bar in Bandra. She drank three pegs of vodka without any effect on her, and Pakya spoke only twice, but Sonawane knew this was his chance.

He can already see the newspaper article: Famous BDD Chawl Buva Proved Innocent Thanks to BDD Chawl Lawyer Sonawane.

A criminal case that hinged on an orchid, a tropical climbing orchid that has fragrant flowers and long podlike fruit, vanilla, Orchidaceae.

'We have chosen you instead of any big criminal lawyer

because you are from the BDD chawls; you know how the residents function, how loyal they are to gangs, how loyal they are to their heroes.'

'Whatever you need, aapko jo kuch bhi chahiye, you ask for it, aap maang lo... Buva baahar aanaa chahiye, Buva must come out, kem?' she had said.

Pakya stared at him with bloodshot eyes, scratching his right arm stump at the elbow with his left.

After she left, after they had piddled together behind the bar on a wall smelling of ammonia, Pakya had barked in street slang, *'Buva aaplya Worli BDD chi shaan hain. Geli tar tumcha kaay hoyil aapun naay saangat.'*

'Buva is the pride of Worli BDD. If that is lost, I can't say what will happen to you.'

Thus it comes to pass that of the two sets of human beings arraigned in the arena of Buva's life, one standing for him and one standing against, Sonawane joins the 'for' set and gets down to battling the labyrinths of the Indian Penal Code.

He jots down, with a sense of detail not too common among his opposing lawyers, the lawyers for the state, the events of the day when Buva climbed up those fateful three floors in Colaba and broke down the door.

Thankfully for him, Pakya is in attendance.

He is allowed to meet Buva and understand his story.

'What time was it?'

'Hmm... the Kamgaar Sabha music was playing, so 11 a.m., when it starts.'

'Why not 11.30 a.m., when it ends?'

'Because I started from Worli at 10.15 a.m. or so... She hadn't paid, so I had gone up to the flat according to instructions given by the darwan.'

'Which floor?'

'Third. It was dark, and at first glance, I thought the door was locked. Then I realised it was a trick. Maybe the guy does that to fool people.'

'Then?'

'I rang the bell, took a chance. He opened the door and said she was not there. That was untrue: I saw her tied to a chair.'

'But why did you break the door?'

'Break the door? No, I broke the chain.'

'Why?'

'Because I rang the bell one more time since I needed my money. My 105 rupees. It was not my concern what he was doing to her.'

'This time he opened the door and pointed a gun.'

'Were you not afraid?'

'I waited till he was about to close the door and then flung myself against it.'

'How did the guy die?'

'Die? I don't know if he died. He was just unconscious, I thought, when I went in. He was lying on the floor. The door must have hit his forehead, or the back of his head may have hit the floor.'

'Why did you shoot him?'

'No, I did not shoot him. I don't know how to use a gun.'

'But you held the gun.'

'Yes, I held the gun.'

'Why?'

'Out of curiosity. I had never held a gun before, despite the many gang wars in our chawls.'

'Why did you say she was a prostitute?'

'Yes, she mentioned this was her job, after I untied her. Somehow, I had missed identifying her, probably because she wore Chanel No. 5, a very sophisticated perfume... Yes, for some strange reason, I had waited for the girl to return. I felt bad about the way she was treated.'

'Treated?'

'Her legs were tied to the chair. Her hands were tied behind her back, and her mouth gagged by bank notes. She was weeping. Her kajol was running down her face.'

'Despite the fact that she was a prostitute, she is a human being.'

'I have known other prostitutes who were kind as human beings to me.'

'So why shouldn't I be kind to them?'

'So you waited until what time?'

'No, I don't remember the time when she returned.'

'And what did she say?'

'Nothing.'

'And where did you drop her off?'

'I had dropped her off at Worli Naka.'

'You noticed anything different about her?'

'Yes, she had a different smell.'

'Different smell?'

'Yes, when she went in, she was wearing Chanel No. 5; when she came back she smelled like vanilla ice cream. I told you... Sorry, I told Jeroo madam.'

'Yes, she told me too. That means she was involved in placing the body of Stanley in the ice-cream freezer. What else?'

'I think she was carrying a rucksack, which I don't think she carried when she went to the house.'

'A rucksack?'

'Probably heavy, because she was bent forward.'

This is when Pakya looks up at Buva and whispers, 'Karim?'

Twenty-three

The Law is a Gentle Geriatric

Time moves slowly in the law courts of India.

There are an estimated over three crore or three hundred million cases pending in multiple levels of courts, translating into millions of stories of human destinies destroyed, adolescence scorched, patriarchy confirming its hyena-hold on justice.

Thankfully, Sinclair D'Souza's desire to make his brother's death in an ice-cream freezer newsworthy has put pressure on the criminal courts.

He feeds and the local TV channels and afternoon dailies

dutifully feast on the contrasting streams of information. The individuals involved are interesting enough to fuel sensationalism and higher circulation and higher viewership for months.

The Ice Cream Murder Case with a multicoloured cast that spans not just Eye Nation and Ear Nation but also Grasse and London!

What more do you need? Bollywood with a Hollywood twist!

Stanley, the benefactor with a heart of gold, helping the hapless (but attractive, woohoo!) widow Sylvia with her children's education.

Photograph: a grainy old image of Sylvia, husband Vernon (with Photoshopped halo to connote dead person) and two young children.

Stanley, the high-end bootlegger and cocaine supplier, friend of Mumbai's hot young Bollywood wannabe stars.

Photograph: muscular young men and pouting young girls on a yacht in Mumbai harbour, Stanley in a Hawaiian shirt, white shorts and straw hat, toasting Mumbai harbour's famed sunset with a huge mug of beer!

Sinclair D'Souza, multimillionaire from London, who defied his parents and his older brother, abandoned his family's illicit businesses and created his own fortune in a foreign land following his own ethics.

Sinclair D'Souza, the conscience-stricken younger sibling, sorrowful, returning for retribution for the family he wronged.

'I merely seek justice. My brother did not hurt anybody ever... so why did this cab driver kill him?'

Photograph: outline of Stanley's body looking like a stiffened embryo in rigor mortis (Caption: As a family newspaper, we refrain from displaying disturbing images as the body was extracted from the ice-cream freezer.)

Buva, the strapping giant, who could end entire gang wars with his steel rod.

Where is he from and why did he kill Stanley for just rupees 105?

Photograph: Buva, in a stained white safari suit, standing, head bowed, as he is carried out of prison to the court.

Jeroo Jeejebhoy, one of India's most famous olfactory scientists, once leading the labs at India's leading cosmetics brand, now hired by one of the world's best cosmetics brands, to create the new range of olfactory experience for millennials around the world.

Why did she wear a Jaipur foot? Why was she estranged from her brother?

Photograph: Jeroo Jeejebhoy at a get-together in the showroom of the cosmetic brand, tall, statuesque, leaning to her right as she smiled at the camera.

Why was she so interested in a cab driver's murder case that she returned from France overnight and was meeting Buva and his lawyer as many times as possible?

A few old-fashioned journalists dig further into the Jeejebhoy connection and come up with interesting gems. The Jeejebhoy family was among nine landowners said to control a fifth of Mumbai's habitable area, close to fourteen thousand acres. 'So what?' is never answered.

Watch this space: Why did she actually choose the lawyer herself? An unknown lawyer with a BDD chawl childhood?

Inspector Prakash Pethe, known to have risen out of the slime of the same BDD chawls, having created his escape velocity with the help of Buva the cab driver now turned against his mentor.

Photograph: Inspector Pethe being honoured at a police function.

Ingrate, bought over by Sinclair, example of one more law upholder now a victim of filthy lucre!

Inspector Prakash Pethe, who studied under streetlights and rose to become one of the most incorruptible cops, now doing his duty, not flinching in arresting his own mentor turned murderer!

Shameful nexus between law protectors and lawbreakers!

Thankfully, Dilshan and his mother Fatima and Ramesh Joshi are nowhere in the media stories.

So when Lawyer Sonawane presents to the court his list of witnesses, the high profile government lawyer, Ujwal Shinde, is taken aback.

As it is, the media has pitched the case as a caste case once again: Maratha government lawyer Shinde versus Dalit Buva lawyer Sonawane. Which lawyer will find justice for his own caste?

And unfortunately, all Shinde's team has done is follow the trajectories of the names mentioned in newspapers and TV, interesting as they are, leading to bizarre conspiracy theories.

Was Jeroo Jeejebhoy involved in a cover-up because Stanley's fridge hid formulae she had smuggled from her Indian employer illegally to her new employer in Grasse?

Was Buva acting on behalf of Prakash Pethe, his BDD chawl friend, who was about to be exposed by Stanley?

Why had his team not known about the role of these stray witnesses?

Compared to murder cases that drag on because of lack of witnesses, the Ice Cream Murder Case sets a record of sorts, in the speed with which it reaches a conclusion against the state despite the star lawyer Ujwal Shinde.

Because of Lawyer Sonawane, who has imbibed the BDD chawls in his subconscious.

The first task Sonawane has set for himself is to get Buva out on bail.

Surprisingly, that is easier done than planned.

The judge is overwhelmed by the witnesses.

A frail coughing Ramesh Joshi is bent over, using the witness stand for support: Maharashtra's most controversial yet most respected playwright, lungs transformed into lacework of black by cancer, yet willing to stand up for Buva.

His wife, Mai, sits upright in the court benches, a huge red bindi on a forehead where the lines of destiny are rewritten by a son who abandoned them, in the same orange sari as when Buva met her first.

The media goes berserk.

A literary giant, willing to come to court, despite his cancer, in support of a cab driver.

'Your Honour, as I said to Buva, cancer is of two types: one that affects the body, and one that affects the heart. I suffer from the first, but Buva's kindness can cure even the second. I believe he is incapable of hurting even an ant. Trust my instinct, sir.'

The second witness is Fatima Sheikh, still in purdah, pushing her thirteen-year-old Dilshan towards her husband in the audience, as she struggles into the witness box, battling her memories of that traumatic afternoon.

'Your Honour, there were three men with swords who

wanted to kill my baby Dilshan… my third, my only surviving baby…'

She pauses, her throat constricted by the flood of memories triggered by her angel friend Buva, standing silent in the criminal box, with his head bowed, wearing the same white safari suit.

She sobs like a child, pauses to catch her breath and blurts '… wanted to kill him… and me.'

The sword raised by the third man distorted by the cab window glass, his hand trying to open the door she has hopefully locked, her heart pounding, mind screaming against the injustice and futility of it all, and then the man turning to look at his fellow killers and magically running away!

'Your Honour, I did not know he was known as Buva… he did not even take the money I wanted to give him… Buva said all mothers are sacred… then, then just drove away… Your Honour, he can't kill for money… who is saying this? Sir, please let him go, I beg you. He is a farishta, not a murderer.'

Ujwal Shinde counters with his own witnesses.

First up is Inspector Wagle of the Colaba Police Station, who recorded the FIR against Buva.

'What was the reason for admitting the FIR against Buva?'

'There were three solid witnesses: the darwan, Santosh Singh, who saw him go up to retrieve his money, the man from the restaurant Kailash Parbat, who said he waited till the lady had returned, and most important, Sylvia herself, who was in the room when Buva killed Stanley.'

'And after we arrested him, his fingerprints matched with those on the gun.'

Unfortunately, Sylvia's FIR statement, presented by Lawyer Sonawane, does not hold up Inspector Wagle's misstatement.

'No, I did not see him kill Stanley. I was blindfolded by Buva and tied to a chair, and he put my handkerchief in my mouth.'

Lawyer Sonawane: 1

Ujwal Shinde: 0

Sonawane pleads to the court, 'There is zero evidence of Buva being violent or money hungry. He has no criminal record.'

'He is known to be a kind, compassionate person. He has never stolen anything in his life. Even the book-selling boys at traffic signals will tell you, he is the only cab driver who allows them to travel with him from one signal to the next.'

'There is no eye witness to prove he killed Stanley.'

'It was Stanley who had the pistol. Most important,

there is no bullet hole in Stanley's body. The pistol has no role to play in this case. It is a Red Herring in legal terms, Your Honour.'

'We plead not guilty. We believe he has been set up, and Buva deserves a proper hearing. Till then, we request bail for Buva.'

'He will appear before court whenever Your Honour wishes him to.'

The court refuses to drag the hearing further. It is sufficiently convinced that there is no conclusive evidence or history of criminal behaviour on Buva's part.

Buva is granted bail.

Twenty-four

Buva and His Return

It's been just twelve months since that fateful dawn when BDD chawls' own son, Prakash Pethe, arrested its own hero, Buva.

Today, Buva returns. Not entirely free from the convoluted clutches of law, but free from a demeaning life in prison.

Sushitai and Shalini have taken control: they don't want what the men want. No shouting, no dancing, no loud music, nothing that decreases the dignity of the man who looked after everyone who needed looking after.

From Annie Besant Road to Worli BDD chawls, there is a corridor of human beings. Not wearing any particular dress, not wearing any badges. Just men and women who felt they had been touched by the compassion of Buva.

At the gate of his building stand the people who refuse to disbelieve his integrity.

Jeroo madam is, to everyone's pleasant surprise, unrecognisable in a sari, dazzling blue and green, perfectly draped, accompanied by a handcrafted blouse. She looks like a queen, tall and unrelenting. Buva tries to touch her feet, but she won't allow it. She hands him one more Swarowski decanter, this time with a top note of courage, and puts the chain around his neck.

Inspector Prakash Pethe, who does not give a fuck what the world thinks after his exposure to the filth and lies in the media, waits in his civil clothes, in a white kurta pyjama, carrying a garland of marigold, which he drapes around Buva's neck and then bends and clutches his feet.

Then they hug and have a conversation without words.

'I'm sorry, Buva, I'm sorry... you taught me not to compromise my integrity in my job, even for those whom I love... that is all I did.'

'It's okay, my brother, it's okay. We don't have to excel in every exam in our lives.'

Pakya, who will hack to death anybody who even doubts

his own Amitabh Bachchan, leaps up in the air, wraps his arms, one strong, one half, around Buva's neck and hugs his hero, tears streaming down his face.

Who is a Dada, a gangster boss?

One who is not bothered about his future. And a new definition: one who sobs publicly only once in a lifetime.

A grinning Sonawane earns many 'taplis' of appreciation, obviously none as violent as the one suffered by the policemen who had come to arrest Buva.

Shalini abandons her reserve and hugs Buva and sobs, 'Don't go away again, please, Buva, don't go… I am so scared.'

Buva is silent and still, his hand on her head, the ignominy of being in jail has created tiny invisible cuts, but he can feel the cooling balm of affection.

The people peel off, as he approaches his room.

He settles down in his room, his nostrils free of offending smells, and for the first time in many years, closes the door of his home.

He reaches under Swami Samarth Ramdas's photograph, extracts the old Swarowski miniature decanter and takes off the cap: oakmoss, musk and sandalwood.

Deep inside him, the fragrance returns him to his time in Shivthar Ghal. The white sound of the waterfall, the grey light in the cave, the darkness of his room.

Somewhere in the memory, though, is a warning, by an old lady, near the waterfall.

Then he gently uncorks the new Swarowski decanter.

Rosemary at the top, eucalyptus in the middle and peppermint at the bottom.

All mood lifters, all happy and sunshiny.

She congratulates him for staying positive despite his trials.

She wants him to be happy despite his tribulations.

Thank you, Jeroo Madam.

Buva's inner-thigh muscles scream as he attempts to perform kurmaasan.

He goads himself, 'Remember, you have done this for decades,' and slowly reaches some semblance of the pose.

Then, as if by miracle, a soft weight lands on his back and pushes him down further.

Kalya.

Buva imagines him sitting with his eyes closed in contentment and smiles.

Do cats feel sad?

Did Kalya feel sad?

Does it matter?

My black friend is back.

How to tell you how much I missed you in jail?

As Buva slowly returns to an upright position, Kalya jumps off, and Buva picks him up.

Buva rubs his beard on his head, as Kalya scrunches his eyes and generates a steady purr in his silken voice box.

Excuse me, human being, can I have a pact with you, of you not vanishing for twelve months?

Apologies, cat, these were circumstances beyond my control.

Twenty-five

The Vanilla Ice Cream Case

Everybody in the media wants to bite off a piece of Buva's flesh.

How odd.

A Dalit cab driver who can quote Swami Samarth Ramdas. But what caste was Swami Samarth Ramdas? We don't know. Maybe a Brahmin.

How strong.

A mere cab driver who can perform 108 surya namaskars instead of the potbellied garden variety we deal with every day.

How strange.

A cab driver who smells so sophisticated like sandalwood, while the rest smell of dry sweat.

How unique.

A slum-dwelling cab driver who has a global leader in perfumery backing him upfront, without any apparent stakes in his life.

'So tell us, Mr Dahire, why you were at the crime scene on 24th April last year?'

'Crime scene? No. I wasn't at any crime scene. I had dropped a passenger, who did not have the money to pay me. So she said she would go to her friend and bring back my money.'

This is probably the longest sentence Buva has uttered in his life.

'Does this happen in your life as a cab driver or is this an exception?'

'Yes. This happens once a year or so. Sometimes, even so called posh people cheat us. Nothing surprising.'

'When this happens, you go up to the place and break down the door?'

'Objection, Your Honour, my esteemed colleague is asking leading questions.'

'Objection upheld. Please stick to a proper line of enquiry, Mr Shinde, or we will shut down the cross-examination.'

'Sorry, Your Honour.'

'So, Buva, is it okay to call you Buva instead of Mr Dahire?'

'Yes.'

'So, Buva, when you went up to the fourth floor...'

'No, third...'

'How are you so sure?'

'Because the darwan said go to the third floor. I didn't know which floor she had gone to; he knew.'

'But you did not know which flat, so how did you go to the correct door?'

'Because all other flats had padlocks; this was the only one unlocked. And there was cool air leaking from below the door.'

'Why did you break down the door?'

'I didn't break down the door.'

'But the police FIR says the chain of the door was broken.'

'Objection, Your Honour, there is no connection between the chain of the door being broken and my client's behaviour... the chain could have always been broken.'

'Objection sustained. Please present a more coherent argument, Mr Shinde.'

'So, Buva, what happened when you reached that door?'

'I rang the bell. One man wearing a towel opened the door, but it had a protective chain holding it only six inches open. I told him one girl had come in my cab and had said she would pay me the cab money after borrowing it from him.'

'He said, no, no girl had come.'

'Then?'

'Before he closed the door, I saw her in the room behind him…. She was tied to a chair. She was gagged. I knew he was lying.'

'But why break the door?'

'I did not break the door. I rang the bell again. He opened the door with a gun in his hand.'

'Is this the man?'

Ujwal Shinde shoves a blown-up photograph of the victim before Buva.

'Yes. He said, fuck off, nikal jao. So I hit the door with my shoulders before he could close it. The chain broke. I wanted to save her.'

'You were angry because he insulted you, so you hit him on his head with the gun?'

'No. His head must have hit the floor. But he was alive. He was breathing.'

'So you took all the cash and ran away?'

'No. I untied the girl from the chair. The girl gave the

money from his wallet, and told me this was her job. She was crying.'

'But you also took all the money lying on the sofa?'

'No, I don't know what money you are talking about. She gave me much more than the 105 rupees she owed me. That's why I waited for her to return. I could drop her off where she wanted to go. She was hurt.'

'No, you waited for her so you could threaten her.'

'Objection, Your Honour, leading question, again... there is no proof that he threatened anybody.'

'Mr Shinde, please provide evidence or hold your statements.'

'Sir, I would like to present witness Sylvia Pereira.'

'Ms Pereira, can you identify the man standing before you?'

'Yes. He dropped me to Colaba last year. To Pasta Lane.'

'Why are you so sure? One year ago?'

'Because of what happened that day. Also, he looks different from normal cab drivers.'

'What happened? '

'I didn't have the 105 rupees I had to pay him for the cab ride. So I said I will go up and get it from our family... Stanley, my late husband's friend.'

'Did you tell him who your friend was?'

'No.'

'Then how did he reach your friend's door?'

'I don't know.'

'When he rang the bell, what happened?'

'I was talking to my friend, our family friend Stanley; he opened the door with the chain on. He told him to wait. But this man broke the chain by hitting the door… Stanley fell on the floor.'

'Fell?'

'He hit his head hard. He fell back, no!'

'Then?'

'Stanley sometimes dealt with rowdy fishermen gangs… so he had a licensed gun. This man saw the gun lying on the sofa, picked it up and threatened me with it.'

'Threatened how?'

'He said, if I told anybody about what had happened, ever told anybody, he would shoot me and my son and daughter.'

'Then?'

'Then he tied me to a chair, blindfolded me. Gagged me.'

'Then?'

'After some time, he took off my blindfold, and again waved the gun at me.'

'Your Honour, Exhibit A, the gun with Buva's fingerprints confirmed by forensics.'

'Then?'

'He told me to come down in five minutes after he had left the flat and enter the cab. He said he would drop me where he had picked me up.'

'Thank you, Your Honour. No further questions.'

'Mr Sonawane, witness is yours for cross-examination.'

'Ms Pereira, do you know this man?'

Sonawane presents a photograph of Santosh Singh.

'Yes.'

'Who is he?'

'He looks like the security guard at the building where Stanley lived.'

'Do you know his name?'

'No.'

'Thank you, Your Honour. No further questions.'

'I would like to call my witness, Karim Khan.'

'Karim bhai, can you explain to the court your profession?'

'I'm a money lender.'

He pauses a bit.

'We lend money without asking for surety, what you call collateral, hai na?'

'Do you know the accused, Buva?'

'Yes.'

'How?'

'I use his cab when I am in Mumbai, when I collect. He stands guard... when I collect cash that is. It is in his cab.'

'Did you trust him with your cash?'

'Yes. That's why we have been working together for twelve years. Lakhs, thousands, crores... he doesn't bother. He doesn't talk much. He is a good man. In our language we call him, Pakhtoon Dil. His heart is like us, like Afghanis, clean, simple.'

'Do you know this man?'

Sonawane presents a photograph of Santosh Singh once again.

'Yes.'

Sinclair D'Souza, London multimillionaire and brother of Stanley, stops smiling for the first time. Pakya watches his reaction with glee.

Between an incoming tide and an outgoing tide, there is lull of thirteen minutes.

Sonawane has waited for the imaginary lull in the minds of the people in the court to get over.

The tide is turning: this is no longer an open and shut case, as made out to be by the media.

'How do you know him?'

'Yes. Santosh Singh. He said he is a security guard in Colaba. He met one of my network of Afghani money lenders, my junior helper. He wanted us to use his cash to make more cash.'

'How much did he bring?'

'Twenty lakhs.'

There is a collective gasp in the courtroom.

'Did you not ask him where he got that much cash?'

'No, sir, our business does not run on questions. It runs on the given word. If you break our trust, you pay more than the money you owe us.'

'So do you keep his address, phone number, anything?'

'Phone number. Sometimes when we suspect something, we do something more. In his case, we suspected there was a risk associated with his cash… very rarely people bring so much first time.'

'What is the risk, then?'

'Because he was coming to us for the first time, we kept his finger prints.'

'Can you share them with us?'

From his wallet in his long-flowing kurta come out two pieces of Sellotape with two fingerprints between them.

'Your Honour, I wish to submit to the court that if the motivation for murder was money, then Santosh Singh is the true culprit who stole the cash from Stanley's flat. I wish to change his status and Sylvia Pereira's status from witness to prime accused….'

Twenty-six

The Unravelling

With a little encouragement from Prakash Pethe, his friends in the police department put Santosh Singh under severe physical stress, which is a euphemism for old-fashioned torture.

There is an underlying current of betrayal: a local Marathi-speaking hero has been made a scapegoat by a Hindi-speaking migrant.

There is an inherent irony in this division, because the earlier division of caste has got whitewashed, and a new layer of regional and linguistic division is operational.

Santosh Singh has been a child of good fortune.

His good looks have allowed him to bypass the usual tests that Mumbai sets up for its migrants. His ability to be well-groomed and polite has added to his charm.

Everything has come easy, including an easy job in a swanky part of town, an unexpected dose of sex with a woman desired by big shots, and now, unheard of cash.

He doesn't have the will or inclination to endure punishment.

Over decades, the Mumbai police has experimented with and perfected tactics of torture that don't show up in medical reports. Thick sticks slapping the soles of feet send shock waves through the body, but leave little evidence. His screams are throttled by his own dirty socks stuffed in his mouth. His lungs burst in pain because his screams can't release his breath. His sobs in the interval bring tears from his eyes.

He attempts to be brave, and sobs, 'Muzhe kuch nahin maalum. Buva ko maalum.'

'I don't know anything. Only Buva knows.'

There is something else that twists the last resistance from him: none of the policemen say anything. They let him do all the talking.

Human beings can survive without food for longer than they can without water than they can without breathing.

Hung upside down by his ankles using bedsheets so

there are no marks on his ankles, thumbs held together by rubber bands behind his back so there are no lasting marks on his hands, Santosh Singh's head is gently lowered in a bucket of water. He thrashes for a panicky minute and a half, and then just when he is about to lose consciousness, returns to earth with monstrous gulps of air.

None of the policemen ask him anything.

Just when he is about to repeat, 'Muzhe kuch nahin…' his head is lowered into the bucket. His words choke him physically and mentally; he never knew such a thing was possible.

His beleaguered mind explodes into images; they have no sequence, no logic, no linkages.

Childhood images from his village in Azamgarh, in Uttar Pradesh: his first leap into a river holding his older brother's hands, the bubbles surrounding his terrified face.

Adolescent images from Mumbai, being insulted by the locals as 'chikna', somebody grabbing his backside.

Grown-up images with Sylvia, locked in impossible poses only a whore would know, all the softness, and the consummate release of passion.

When he emerges in the sea of air, he knows he has lost the battle.

'Chhod do, mujhe jeene do.'

His gasps are huge, trying to suck as much air as possible.

Release me, I wish to live.

Prakash Pethe makes sure there are no more slip-ups.

Santosh Singh's testimony to the police is video recorded.

He admits working with Sylvia Pereira.

Their mobile phone records are drilled into, revealing interesting dates, days and times.

He submits other details.

When Stanley was not in town, Sylvia and Santosh had enjoyed a sexual encounter in the air-conditioned comfort of his flat. Two individuals had discovered an easy route to extend their easy cravings. So easy that Santosh did not mind being a partner in crime.

By sheer luck, Buva had landed on the day that Stanley got all his collections laid out on the bed.

Almost in slow motion, like watching a spider spin its web in rewind, Sonawane takes apart the silken threads woven around Buva and then step-by-careful-step, proves how Santosh Singh and Sylvia Pereira had planned and worked together for many months for an opportunity.

Sylvia had called him after Buva left, and both of them had stuffed the unconscious (or dead?) Stanley into the giant ice-cream freezer.

She had stuffed the cash into a sack, the sack that she did not have when she had entered the building, and which Buva remembered.

Santosh had then taken the cash from her later during the week and cleverly, instead of splurging it and drawing attention to themselves, tried to earn interest on it.

The fingerprints with Karim Khan matched Santosh Singh's fingerprints.

Twenty-seven

Blooming Rose to
Venus Trap

S ylvia smiles in her dreams.

She is standing before Vernon in the Vasai Fort, as he dances on the walls doing the Sylventine, the sun blinding her ricocheting off the sea.

He smiles indulgently at her, but this time she can see the future of his deceit.

She smiles back, no, she laughs, for the first time in her life; she experiences a certainty of outcome.

She pushes him off the wall.

She can't come to terms with the words that emerge in her mind.

'Bastard, you made love to me as your wife while you were converting me into a whore.'

Vernon falls in slow motion; she is terrified he will never reach the bottom, or he will fall in the water and survive, and come back to auction her body.

Thankfully for her, Vernon falls on rock, on his head, then slips into the sea and rises up, with a huge banner behind him that has three letters: DOA.

She watches Stanley on the deck of his luxury yacht, Hawaiian shirt and straw hat, grabbing her around her waist.

'He's gone, babes. It's now you and me.'

This time, she has the kitchen knife from his enormous Colaba kitchen in her hand.

How? Dreams have no 'how'.

For some reason, she is able to slide it into his big stomach so easily, she can't believe she had thought his tummy was hard under his tight T-shirt.

'Stanley, you killed my husband and then made me a whore… what's a knife into your stomach?'

'Hahahahaha!'

Her kids are afraid of her now. She no longer kisses them every morning. She no longer asks them if they like the tiffin she gives them.

She is on the phone, talking to someone, but she is very stern.

They have a new mom.

In her dreams every night, the Shrinking Violet morphs into a Blooming Rose and then turns into a Venus Trap.... An untutored ego is unable to bear the burden of an orphaned childhood, an abandoned youthful marriage, and being the prey in a sexual predatory game.

You can't fling me out like a used condom. I never signed up for this.

She hides the cocaine in her purse and gets it home: it becomes the white stream of consciousness, extending from the glass on which she makes the lines into her nostrils into the multiple spongy canals inside her brain, each one leading to a darker dream.

The criminal case against Sylvia Pereira and Santosh Singh is swallowed whole by a boa constrictor known as the Indian legal system. Sylvia and Santosh end up undertrials in the same prison that Buva had been, dehumanised by the experience until they no longer care.

Sylvia grows deranged, unable to cope with the cocktail of hope, despair, triumph, shame and defeat, all her anchors gone.

Thankfully, Vernon's brother from Vasai agrees to adopt the orphans, who never see their mother again.

Twenty-eight

The River Dies

I n February 2018, the first Slum Rehabilitation Project involving the BDD chawls in Sewree kicked off.

Five thousand families were shunted to temporary shelters, and the impassive stone walls imploded under carefully placed dynamite.

A theatre of history reduced to rubble.

The end of history.

The history of the Konkan belt providing eighty percent of the grist of labourers to the mills of Bombay.

The history of the British plan to create large-scale prisons for the mounting number of rebels in India.

The history of caste wars of the fiercest kind.

The history of wars between criminals versus the state law machinery.

The history of strangers becoming blood brothers and blood brothers becoming strangers.

The history of fathers becoming rapists and orphans becoming stars.

The BDD chawls in Worli wait patiently for their turn, all its twenty-six acres, graceful old ficus religiosa veterans and 120-odd buildings, as the government machinery grinds slowly, waiting for a hundred bureaucrats to bite off their pound of flesh from this huge infrastructure project cost.

Greed knows neither caste nor class.

Years after Buva has returned, he is waiting outside Bombay Central station, when he spots the usual suspects in white. Rich men from villages, wanting to enjoy the fruits of Mumbai's anonymity.

'From where?' Buva asks casually.

'Khairlanji,' they reply, as they put their rexine bags on the carrier of the Fiat.

A metallic ting begins in Buva's head.

They want to go all the way to Fantasyland in Gorai.

'Don't you remember in our childhood that Dahire family... the bloody father and mother were both turned into charcoal by our villagers? Remember she jumped into a well, so did her husband.'

'Of course,' agrees the other. 'Arre that's the only way to stop this nonsense... these gutter worms trying to raise their heads... but here in the cities na... too much police follow up...'

Their khik-khik giggle is like the stuttering car engine that refuses to start on cold mornings.

Buva's breathing is getting a bit ragged, the silken rhythm set by the twenty-four surya namaskars in the morning shredded by the idea of the abyss he is planning to enter.

The two passengers are unaware of the change within Buva; they are busy recounting the tales of their native village, their conversation now punctuated by laughter.

'Ae driver, can you arrange for a place with some chhammak chhallos?'

Buva's response is a shake of the head, and a choked 'Sure, haan, hmm,' thinking meanwhile of a mother running towards a well with no water, trailing flames.

I need a plan, I need a plan. His nose detects the heavy smell of attar and an idea sprouts in his mind.

'Do you want to go slightly out of town, only one-and-a-half hours, away from police and people, nice swimming pool... like that? They have all choices... model women, actresses, nice?'

The two men in the back seat do not realise he is talking to them.

'What?'

'Slightly out of town, only one and a half hours? They have all choices... model women, actresses, good rates.'

'You know?'

'Yes, I take a friend, client, every year, for ten years...'

You can even get a transvestite, like my friend did, if you fancy one, he added in his mind, trying to control the metallic ting in his left temple.

'OK, how much?'

'I go by the meter, take you, bring back. You negotiate with hotel for everything else. Meter will be six to seven hundred rupees plus waiting charges.'

'This is not a trap, is it?'

Well, it is, but not the type you are expecting.

No, Buva, you can't let the river run on.

Just as his guru ran away from the wedding ceremony right before he was to be garlanded by the bride when the priest shouted 'Savdhaan', 'Attention, pay attention', Buva must return from the brink of the river of hate.

They reach Kismet Resort around 4 p.m. Buva's nose remembers the smell of the Ghodbunder creek as he drives on the bridge over it.

But the resort manager, Pratap, has discouraging news.

The girls will arrive only by 5 p.m. It is too early. They come from all parts of town, reach the railway station at Bhayender, and then take a rickshaw.

Buva suggests an alternative. There is a beautiful Durga temple across the highway, on the other side, but you need to climb a bit.

'It's very old and very beautiful,' agrees Pratap. 'By the time you return, the girls will be here.'

The Brahmins from Khairlanji, wrapped in their starched white kurtas, look at each other.

'OK... let's meet the real goddess before we meet the fake goddesses.' Their giggles are getting breathless.

The Durga temple is indeed very old, built out of solid stone, probably carved out of a monolithic rock, and behind it stand rock walls where sometimes the young rock-climbers of Mumbai pit their muscles against nooks and crannies and cracks.

Around the temple are two square water tanks, still half-full, their fifteen-odd feet walls smooth with moss, opportunistic ficus trees feeling up the cracks with their roots, the water at the bottom reflecting slices of the sky or the darkness of the walls.

Buva is sweating now, almost deafened by the metallic ting in his forehead, for what he is planning to do is scaring him and angering him simultaneously.

The white-cocooned duo have done their namaskars before the goddess and walked around the temple thrice, keeping the goddess to their right, clockwise, always clockwise, as they have been trained since childhood.

They spot Buva sitting by the tank, his feet dangling over the edge, staring at the rock wall behind the temple.

'What's there?' they ask him.

'Sit here, you can see...' he says as he stands up, offering his seat to them.

'See what?'

'My past.'

'What?'

They lower themselves next to the edge of the tank, grunting at the task of getting their bellies out of the way, unmindful of the stains their sinless whites will pick up.

Buva's mind is sitting on a huge swing, making him giddy: anger, hate, anger, hate, no, they are not responsible, no they are, they enjoy trampling other human beings, but they did not push your mother, no they did, their brethren did, they are all the same butchers.

'Ae, driver, what did you say... see on the wall?'

When he pushes them, they scream.

He has waited for decades to hear those screams.

But their screams are short, not as long as his mother's

scream—it does not last forty years, inside the caves inside his head, laced by the stench of burning flesh.

Their screams have ended in twin splashes, and the water embraces their starched white cocoons, and they gasp as the coldness enters their orifices.

They are not swimmers, so they thrash about in panic. Thankfully, the water is neck level high, and very soon, still gasping, they reach the sides of the tank, clutch the roots of the ficus.

Those irritating khik-khik giggles are replaced by ha-ha of large gulps of air being swallowed and as the fact that they will not die sinks in, they look up and shout, 'Ae are you mad...'

'Maadarchod,' he can hear himself roar now, his eyes stinging with tears held back for forty years, 'that woman your village set on fire, that woman was my mother, understand? My mother! You fucking bastards... she was my mother.'

'Maadarchod, imagine how it feels to fall in a well without water! Imagine!'

For a minute, there is silence. The starched duo wait in the cold water in terror, not knowing what to do next, absorbing this strange information.

So this giant was the son of that female pig their parents had set on fire forty years ago. Damn our luck.

Just to dissolve all the knots in his mind and heart, Buva goes away from the tank, picks up a boulder and stands by the edge of the tank.

'Want to set fire to any more mothers?'

He holds the boulder above his head. The duo cannot see his expression, but his silhouette is clearly etched against a blue sky.

'No! Please no... maaf kar... pardon us... we did not do anything,' they scream and gibber. When one of them folds his hands in supplication, he goes under water for a moment, and then lunges to grab the ficus root.

'Take this, you bastards!' says Buva and flings the boulder down.

It lands away from them, behind them, creates waves that reach their nostrils, and they gasp again and plead and gibber again.

'No, no, please don't kill us, please, think of our children...'

Think of our children.

Think of our children.

That's when the blackness parts within Buva, and he understands for the first time in four decades the exact detail he had suppressed: his mother was pregnant when she ran into the well. He would have been an elder brother to someone. He would not have been alone in life. He would not have been the ant that strayed from the hill.

Think of our children.

She was pregnant when she jumped into that waterless well, like Reshma was when HIV caught up with her.

It's all so hopeless, this unending spiral of hate.

The metallic ting in his ears increases, and the gush of tears dries up.

You were arrested wrongly for murder, now you don't want to get arrested rightly for two.

'Jethe jaaneev to satvaguna, madhye to rajoguna, naneev tamoguna, jaaneje shroti.'

'Remember,' says Swami, 'awareness is the quality of satva and light, non-awareness leads to tamas and darkness.'

He flings rock after rock at the hapless duo, making sure he doesn't hit them, just to make them piss in fear in the water.

By the time he has finished flinging six rocks, that roar in his head is replaced by emptiness.

He turns around and walks down the slope, away from the temple, towards Kamandalu, his chest straining against the white, sobbing empty sobs, the whole damn catastrophe of life: desire, whether to help others or in one's selfish interest, carried within itself the roots of frustration.

There is only one real enemy: desire.

It is time to return to Shivthar Ghal.

Epilogue

Madam Jeejebhoy sat in the balcony of her flat overlooking the shimmering bay of Mumbai.

This sea is very different from the sea in Bordi.

This one rushes at you, eager to wrap itself around your feet if you are standing, wetting your backside if you are sitting, inviting, imploring, come and merge with me.

That one kept ebbing away, shying away from human touch, retreating over acres of lonely sand, reluctantly allowing a distant moon to tumefy its gun-metal bosom.

Had Madam Jeejebhoy run away from a brother who blamed her and now she had somehow, in saving Buva's life, found redemption?

Was Buva the brother she yearned to have: quiet, accepting, always there?

She didn't know why exactly but she felt calmer than she had ever felt before.

Why argue against yourself?

She decided to return to Grasse, to her professional home, to the festivals of fragrance, to the intoxicating art of merging the East and the West, for good.

After Buva retired to Shivthar Ghal, Pakya and Shalini got into a partnership, where he offered bhaji and vada pao, street food of Mumbai, next to her juice stall. Tongues set on fire by garlic and chilli chutney are doused by lemon or orange or mango or chikoo juice.

Far away, Buva sat cross-legged behind the roar of the waterfall; his only umbilical cord to the BBB chawls is Kalya, his black cat, who lay on his back next to him.

How many rivers pass through how many living beings in how many ways?